D1488127

CHANGE OF HEART

Tracy Stern

Simon & Schuster

SIMON & SCHUSTER
Rockefeller Center
1230 Avenue of the Americas
New York, NY 10020

SIMON & SCHUSTER and colophon are registered trademarks of Simon & Schuster Inc.

Designed by Irving Perkins Associates

Manufactured in the United States of America

10 9 8 7 6 5 4 3 2 1

Library of Congress Cataloging-in-Publication Data
Stern, Tracy.
Change of Heart / Tracy Stern
p.   cm.
I. Title.
PS3569.T415C48   1997
813'.54—dc21   96-53357 CIP
ISBN 0-684-81121-9

For B. B.
More than ever.

Prologue

"Having a baby at your age should be no problem at all," her grandmother had told her. "In your early twenties it's nothing. A short labor, and that's it. You'll be out of the hospital in no time."

But it hadn't been easy, Kerry thought as she slowly shifted her tortured body, moving from one side to the other in the narrow hospital bed. Everything ached. It had been twelve hours of hard, exhausting labor. The countless urgings from her birth coach to breathe and push, breathe and push, still echoed in her ears.

Cautiously, Kerry raised herself up on her elbows, pushed back the covers, and climbed out of bed. She glanced over at her hospital roommate, an older woman who slept soundly now. The woman's family—a grown son and daughter—had come to visit earlier in the evening, and Kerry was painfully aware of their whispered voices as they glanced in her direction. She sensed they knew why she was there, in a room far away from the maternity ward, far away from the baby she had given birth to only hours earlier. They had looked at her with a combination of interest and pity, and when their eyes met, Kerry had turned her face from them, unable to acknowledge their stares.

The lights in the hallway had been dimmed, giving the corridor an eerie feeling. Kerry checked in both directions before walking toward the elevators. She knew what she was doing was forbidden, but she couldn't resist. She had to see her son.

She approached the nursery's protective glass cautiously, apprehensive, yet filled with excitement. The baby beds stood in rows; there were so many of them. It had been a busy night at the hospital.

Kerry's eyes traveled from newborn to newborn, searching. Will I always be able to recognize him? she wondered. Even if years pass without seeing him, will he always be familiar to me? As her eyes darted from baby to baby, each identically wrapped in a pristine white cloth, she panicked. Which one *was* he? There were so many, and they looked so much alike, yet surely she would know him.

Just when she had nearly convinced herself that something terrible had happened to him, that he was sick, that he had required special care, her eyes locked on a baby in the first row. It was him! He was asleep, but she would know her son anywhere. Then she looked at the crib, and at the card placed at the front of the crib so that visitors would be able to pick out the new addition to their family. She recognized the last name of his new parents. All at once the finality of her decision struck her. It was done. Now there could be no turning back.

Kerry suddenly felt weak, her legs collapsing beneath her. She grabbed on to the ledge at the bottom of the window, trying to break her fall. Nothing, neither the many sessions with the counselor nor the late-night talks with Lisbeth, had prepared her for the overwhelming experience of childbirth. The bond she felt with this tiny infant in the crib before her was so much stronger than she had anticipated, perhaps even as strong as what she still felt for his father.

How will I ever be able to give him up? she wondered. How will I find the strength to keep my promise? In just two days, they will take him away. How will I ever find the strength to say good-bye?

Her questions echoed in her confused mind as she felt the gentle touch of the nurse's hand on her elbow.

"Come, dear, you must go back to your room now," she said softly, guiding her slowly away from the nursery.

Kerry looked back at the crib once more before turning away, then shrugged off the nurse's hand. Oh, Brad, what have I done? she said to herself as she headed slowly back to her bed.

PART
I

Chapter 1

Kerry McKinney loved holidays, especially Christmas. And especially this year. She took great care dressing for Christmas Eve, wanting to look her very best. She had decided to wear her new dress tonight rather than save it for lunch at the Evanses on Christmas Day. Tomorrow's event would be more casual, and a pair of leggings and a sweater would be just fine. Besides, that way she would already be dressed for the drive to the lake with Brad.

Kerry studied her image in the mirror. At five foot nine, she often worried that she was too tall, or that the muscles in her legs were overdeveloped from all the skiing and tennis, but tonight she knew that none of that mattered. Tonight she was pleased with what she saw. She knew also that it wasn't so much the new dress, or even the strand of pearls that had been her graduation present from her grandmother Lisbeth that made her seem different in her own eyes. No, tonight she radiated from the inner glow she wore knowing that she loved and was loved in return. And not just by Brad, although he was, of course, the most important, but by her family and friends as well. And even though Coach could be harsh and unremittingly strict at times, beneath that tough exterior was a father who adored his only daughter. Yes, tonight Kerry felt truly blessed.

After one last twirl of assessment, she hurried downstairs to the kitchen where Nancy, her mother, continued to bustle around, checking last-minute details. Seeing Kerry, she smiled broadly and gave a nod of approval.

"Oh, sweetheart, you look terrific. Turn around." Kerry made the requested spin, playfully, holding out her skirt as she did so. "Great, and your pearls look wonderful against the blue velvet. Grandmother Lisbeth is right, with a good strand of pearls and a good handbag a girl can go anywhere."

"Well, I sure agree about the pearls," Kerry said, catching her reflection again in the kitchen window, "but I'll pass on the handbag, thank you." It's funny, she thought, that her grandmother really was right about so many things. In many ways, even to one as young as Kerry, she seemed to be way ahead of her time. She found her wisdom on a wide range of subjects both thoughtful and valuable.

"And don't forget, we have to call Lisbeth and Charles tonight," her mother said. "I tried once already, but they weren't in. Remind me to call again before it gets too late."

"Okay," Kerry agreed, as she tied an apron around her waist. I should have made the pie before getting dressed, she thought, but there had been too many other things to do earlier in the day. She glanced at the clock. It was nearly six; Brad and her younger brother, Willy, should be on their way back by now, she realized. Even though they had promised to get home in time to help, she knew they would stay away until the last possible moment, then rush into the house just in time to get cleaned up for dinner.

She was in the middle of rolling out the pie crust when she heard the familiar sound of Brad's old VW as he pulled into the driveway. She looked down at the floury mess, unconvinced that a homemade crust really made all that much difference. It would have been so much simpler to buy a frozen one; besides, it *was* Christmas.

"We're back," Willy yelled from the driveway as he crawled out of the tiny car and started pulling out all his ski gear.

"Return of the athletes," Kerry's mother mused as she carried serving pieces out to the sideboard.

"Right on time. What is it about men that gives them a signal just when all the work is done? Must be some secret radar," Kerry declared as she pressed the crust into the pie pan.

"You missed a great day, Sis," Willy said by way of greeting. "I don't remember the snow ever being more perfect. That last run was something else." Kerry smiled as she watched her brother and her boyfriend together. They had become truly good friends, and it thrilled her that her family was as fond of Brad as she was.

"Stay out! Stay completely away from that," Nancy warned as she spotted Willy picking up the lid of the pan containing the wild rice. "Out! Now get upstairs, the others will be here soon. Hurry and get changed. We still have a few chores left for you to do."

Brad had taken time to shower and change at the lodge, and so he looked fresh and handsome in a plaid flannel shirt and gray wool pants. Kerry noticed also that his skin had a healthy glow from his day outdoors, and even above the aroma of the food, she could smell the familiar scent of her favorite cologne.

He smiled brightly at her as he advanced across the kitchen.

"Looking beautiful," he said as he came to a stop beside her. "New dress?"

Kerry took a deep breath, filling her lungs with the sweet scent of him. "Yes it is. I treated myself. Like it?" she asked, although already certain of the answer from the sparkle in his eyes.

"Very much." He stood directly behind her now, peering over her shoulder. She tried to keep her focus on the pie, but just feeling him there almost touching her, made it nearly impossible for her to think of anything other than him. He bent over, nuzzling her neck with his nose, planting soft kisses. The scent of him was overwhelming. Kerry felt her knees weaken with the mere thought of his strong arms around her, and she shook her head vigorously to ward off the overpowering emotion.

"I've got you trapped now, hands in the pie. I could take advantage of you right here and now," he teased, finally touching her with his hands, lifting her hair, kissing the back of her neck.

"Brad, stop it," she said, trying to sound serious. "We've got the whole week ahead of us, but right now I have to get this pie in the oven. So come on now, be good and let me finish this," she urged, twisting her head in an effort to get him to stop.

"I don't care about the pie," he answered, moving closer behind her and wrapping his arms around her. He ran his hands over the apron, brushing his fingertips against her nipples.

"Okay, Brad, that's it," Kerry said, struggling to keep up her resolve. "We're not alone here, you know." She poked him in the stomach with her elbow and tried to wriggle out of his grasp, but the more she squirmed the tighter he held her.

"Oh, really, who's here? I don't see anyone."

Kerry looked around to find that both her brother and mother had indeed left the kitchen. Taking advantage of her turned head, Brad kissed her. "Come on, Kerry," he said. "Just play a little game with me for a minute, and then I'll go away, I promise."

"I know your little games," she said, laughing. Then she sighed. "All right, but just for a minute, and only if you promise to leave me alone and let me finish."

"Okay, close your eyes," he said. "Come on now, you promised."

Kerry closed her eyes, she felt Brad's hands cover hers, and just for spite she rubbed sticky crust and flour all over them.

"I don't want you for only a week," he whispered in her ear. "I want you forever."

Kerry heard his words at the same moment she felt him gently slide the ring over her finger. She smiled tentatively, certain this was only another of his jokes. But when she opened her eyes, she saw a ring with three small diamonds, set in a row, glistening on her flour-covered hand.

"Oh, Brad," she said, trying to catch her breath. She turned to face him, and knew in that instant that she would forever hold his expression in her heart. His smile was so broad, his eyes so filled with love. "It's beautiful . . . it really is," she stammered, holding out her hand.

"Well?"

"Well, what?"

"I've been told that it's not official until you say yes. So please say yes."

Tears suddenly flooded her eyes. "Oh, yes, yes . . . a thousand times yes," she said, turning in his arms and taking his face in her hands. They were still kissing when they heard someone enter the kitchen.

It was Coach. "Kissing again," he commented dryly. "Well, did she agree to your demands?"

Kerry looked at her father quizzically. He smiled and opened his arms to her. Clearly he was in on Brad's scheme. "Congratulations, you two," he said. "I think this really calls for a celebration."

Toasts were made throughout dinner. Kerry looked around the table and, listening to the words of good wishes, she felt truly blessed.

Her grandmother Lisbeth called and was elated to hear

the news. Kerry received her grandmother's good wishes, promising her that she would make a trip to San Francisco with her mother when she was ready to start planning the wedding.

"I might have something in the attic that would be of use to you," Lisbeth said sweetly. "But we can talk about all of that later. Have a wonderful time skiing, dear, and kiss everyone for me."

Lisbeth's call brought the evening to an end. Brad's parents, who were a part of the evening, offered to help clean up, but Brad insisted that they go on home and let him do his share. It was, of course, merely an excuse to be with Kerry for a little while longer, but no one resisted.

When the kitchen was back in order, Kerry and Brad found themselves alone again.

She reached up to caress his face. "Just a moment," he said, taking her hands in his, turning her ring to the light and making the diamonds sparkle.

"Like it?" he asked.

"It's the most beautiful ring, Brad, I love it. Almost as much as I love you," she replied, holding him and pressing her face into his neck.

"Tomorrow, I can't wait for tomorrow," Brad said. "I'll have you all to myself."

"You're going to have me forever," Kerry added, kissing him now, deeply.

"I'm counting on it," he said, stepping back as she helped him on with his ski jacket. "Merry Christmas to the future Mrs. Evans," he added, kissing her lightly on the fore-head. "Oh, and by the way, great pie."

"I'll never be able to make another without thinking of diamond rings," she laughed, then stopped, putting her arms around him again. "Brad," she began, "lots of kids, and a whole pack of dogs, right?"

"And a big house with a big yard," he added. "I'll make all your dreams come true. I promise."

"You've made a good start," she answered. "Merry Christmas."

Chapter 2

The lodge sat at the top of an incline and its wide front lawn sloped to the shore of Lake Tahoe. The entire expanse was covered with a frosty layer of glistening snow, a perfect setting for a Christmas day.

When they first arrived, Kerry went from room to room, surveying the layout and staking out the best room for them. It was certainly an uncharacteristically luxurious sur-rounding for college kids to enjoy. Kerry's mom was the manager of an inn nearby, and they had her to thank for finding the place and making the arrangements with the owners.

Kerry and Brad would have the lodge all to themselves for two days. Then Brad's roommate and his girlfriend would arrive on Saturday. Kerry had strictly forbidden Willy to come anywhere near the place until then.

Shortly after arriving and settling in, the skies darkened and the snow began again.

"Doesn't look too serious," Brad predicted, standing on the upstairs balcony, surveying the lake and the mountains in the distance. "Let's get the groceries put away; I bet we can still have several hours on the slopes."

"Oh, I wouldn't be too sure," Kerry answered, standing behind him, her arms wrapped around his waist. "I think this might last for a while." Secretly she prayed for a blizzard. As much as she loved to ski, she wanted nothing more than to be snowed in with this man whose love for her had taken on a whole new meaning.

Brad turned to her and took her in his arms. "Maybe it wouldn't be so bad, after all, having to stay inside all day," he said, kissing her forehead and slowly working his lips down the side of her face, back up to her temple, down and around her ears, and then finally connecting with her mouth.

Kerry's knees weakened as she urged him closer. With his arms about her, he led her downstairs to the big living room, and in a frenzied effort, built an enormous fire. Then he rushed upstairs to their room and pulled the soft down pillows and comforter from the bed, carrying them back downstairs. Kerry watched from her position on the sofa as he arranged the quilt and pillows, intent on creating a warm and cozy space for them. One of the many things she loved about Brad was his lack of self-consciousness in handling tasks normally associated with women. Unlike most of the men she knew, her brother and father included, he was able to do such things with grace and without being the least bit embarrassed about it. He possessed this same softness and gentle way when he made love to her, a trait which Kerry found overpoweringly masculine.

"For you, my love," he announced gallantly, bending at the waist and beckoning Kerry to join him. "Let it snow!" he proclaimed, easing Kerry into the soft nest he had created.

She surrendered willingly, as he placed her head gently on the soft pillow, then lay down beside her, his eyes never once leaving her face.

She reached over and pulled him to her, and the magic began. His hands in her hair, his face moving from side to side, covering her with whispers of adoration. Her sweater pulled—again gently—over her head, the first in what soon became a heap of clothes. As they undressed, their desire for each other heightened, reaching fever pitch as Kerry raised her hips and allowed Brad to slip his hands beneath her and remove her last piece of clothing. Hungry and impatient now, and filled with the need to feel the power of him inside her, she urged him to take her. She felt her body swept up in a need made even more intense by the lifelong commitment they had made to each other.

Brad hesitated for a moment, torn between wanting to

prolong the sweetness of their lovemaking, and his own urgent desire to have her in the most intimate way. He looked down at her, and sensing the longing in her eyes, decided to give in to his burning physical need. He felt around near the hearth, fumbling for what he knew he had placed there a few minutes earlier. He located the package, and with trembling hands struggled to open the sealed packet. Unsuccessful, he handed it to Kerry. She hesitated, wanting so to feel him inside her without the sheath keeping them apart. But she thought better of it; as much as she hated the protection, it was crucial. Now was not the time for mistakes.

They made love all afternoon, then fell into an exhausted sleep. By the time they awakened, the snow was piled up high outside, night had fallen, and the warmth of the blazing fire was a mere memory.

"If I get more wood on there quickly we may be able to revive it," said Brad, staring into the remaining embers.

"Go ahead, but I'm not moving out from under here," Kerry answered from beneath the down coverlet. "It's freezing."

"Not for long," he assured her, stacking logs and rolling up newspaper to rekindle the blaze. "You'll never be cold with me around," he added.

"I know," she said, smiling and opening her arms to him as he rejoined her under the covers. Kerry melded her body to his, her back against his chest, his belly pressed into the curve of her spine, their legs bent at exactly the same angle. Brad held her close, his hands cupping her breasts from behind. In this most intimate position they drifted off into a peaceful sleep, their dreams filled with the future, oblivious to the storm outside.

Chapter 3

Kerry awakened each morning before Brad. As she lay next to him, she would watch as he slept, watch and dream about their life together. She imagined the children they would have, beautiful, perfect little boys and girls. With her eyes shut she could hear their laughter, could feel their tiny hands in hers, and her own hand would be held in Brad's powerful grasp. They would have such a wonderful life together, loving, supportive of each other. Each new morning, as she lay beside Brad, she thanked God for her good fortune.

Their days alone ended with the arrival of Brad's roommate and his girlfriend, Jennifer, followed by Willy, and then by Brad's youngest sister, Amy.

The days were spent on the slopes, the nights at the fireside enjoying whatever meal Kerry had pulled together for dinner, since she was the only one who had a clue about what to do in the kitchen.

The time passed far too quickly, and on New Year's Eve,

instead of feeling joyous and celebratory, Kerry felt a black mood settle over her. All too soon Brad would be returning to school and she would go back to her own classes and work. She felt melancholy, and it showed.

"Cheer up, Kerry. No more of that sad face," Brad urged as he held her in his arms. They were in their big bed with the covers pulled up around them. Outside the moon's glow reflected off the lake, sending streams of light into the room.

"Besides, we still have two more days, and then I'll be back here before you know it. Only three months until spring break."

"Easy for you to say," she said glumly. "You're down there, in a great city, with a whole new group of friends, and in the meantime, I'm stuck up here in Carson City. I know I promised to stay here for the time being, but sometimes it's so frustrating. I know I have my classes at the junior college, which are interesting, but I feel as if I'm wasting so much of my time in the dead-end job at the insurance company and my waitressing job. I'm anxious to start spending more time on my writing." It was unlike her to complain, and Brad's reaction was to raise himself up on his elbow and give her a hard look.

"That's hardly fair, Kerry. I thought we had a deal. You agreed to everything we're doing. You're right, I am in a new environment, and I have made a new set of friends. But every moment I can I spend with you. It hasn't been easy for either of us. I get worried when I hear you say something like that."

Immediately she felt sorry for what she had said. She

was acting like a spoiled brat. "I'm sorry, I really am," she began. "It's just that sometimes it seems we'll never be together.
The days are endless, and I think they will never pass. Right
now three months is the same as forever to me," she sighed.

"Forever is what we're going to have together," he assured her, turning toward her and stroking her body as they
began to make love.

When they finally cuddled up to each other, their bodies exhausted from the pleasure they had given each other,
Kerry felt that the new year boded well for them, for their future and their life together.

Although she had willed the time to pass slowly, their
vacation still ended much too soon for Kerry.

"Just twelve weeks, look at it that way," Brad tried to
cheer her up as he packed the small trunk of his car and prepared for the drive south.

"I prefer three months, sounds much shorter to me that
way," Kerry responded, smiling, trying to hold back her tears.

"Love you," she whispered in his ear as he prepared to
drive off.

"I love you too. See you soon."

And then he was gone, leaving Kerry to return to her
own studies and work routine. The memories of their holiday
together sustained her from morning until late at night when
she put on Brad's old football jersey and fell asleep, clutching
to her heart the brilliant diamond ring he'd given her.

No matter what her day was like, Kerry made a point
of putting something in the mail to Brad every single day. A
postcard, a funny card, or a quick "I love you" and a lipstick

imprint of a kiss, just so he would have a little reminder of her each and every day.

Every spare moment she had, she spent planning her wedding. She and Brad had agreed on a date in early August because it would leave them enough time for a short honeymoon before they would have to move down to L.A. where Brad would begin his second year of medical school in mid-September.

A typical bride-to-be, Kerry wanted each detail to be absolutely perfect. She spent hours with Brad's sister, Amy, lying on her bed, shoes thrown off, her feet kicking in the air. Every bridal magazine ever published was strewn about the room. Every few seconds one of them would call out, "Look at this! Let's think about this veil, it's a definite possibility!" The page would then be ripped out and added to the stack of serious contenders.

Arriving home dead tired from her job at the restaurant late one night, Kerry was surprised to find a big package on the kitchen table. It was from Lisbeth, a coffee table book about weddings. After Kerry quickly flipped through the pages of beautiful color photographs of all different kinds of weddings, she opened the accompanying letter from her grandmother. Written on thick robin's egg blue stationery in her familiar handwriting, it began:

"My dearest Kerry, it is with much love and wishes for your everlasting happiness that Charles and I send you this book. I hope it will serve as an inspiration as you are planning your own very special day."

Lisbeth went on to recap their holidays, and how

thrilled she was that Charles had been able to make the outing to the club. Kerry read all of this with interest, but she was
especially happy when she came to the end of the letter.

"So, my darling grandchild, I am certain that you will
not be able to find everything you will want in Carson City,
even in Reno for that matter. So, why don't you think about
coming to San Francisco for a long weekend? We can visit the
shops here where there is a much broader selection of all
things necessary for a perfect wedding. It would be such fun
to have you here, that is, if you can fit it into your already busy
schedule. This, of course, would be Charles and my gift to
you. Just let me know when. I'll arrange to have an airline
ticket sent to you, and I'll be waiting at the airport when you
arrive. Hoping to hear that you are coming soon. With love,
Lisbeth."

A trip to San Francisco! How thoughtful of her grandmother. It was certainly a luxury she would never have considered, since she and Brad had promised to save every penny
possible. Kerry was thrilled beyond words. Now all she had
to do was finish a paper for school and arrange for the time
off from work.

"I'm just sorry I can't go with you," her mother said, as
they entered the airport. "But I know you'll have a wonderful time with your grandmother. She's bound and determined to make up for the fact that your father and I chose
not to have a big wedding—or any wedding at all for that

matter. You know we just eloped. Made her crazy for many years. But now you're giving her the chance she never had. She's beside herself.

"You should also talk to her about your career. Lisbeth has been very successful with her writing, and she can help you. Maybe she'll even introduce you to some of the people at the magazine. It's a chance for you to make some connections that might help you in the future."

Kerry smiled at her mother. "You're right. I've thought about that too. She's offered in the past, and now I can take her up on it. Still, I wish you were coming. But I know it's impossible. Tahoe hasn't had a season this good in years. Is it true the inn is booked all the way through April?"

"Absolutely, it hasn't been this good in a decade. You and Lisbeth will do fine without me. Just let me know when you're coming home, and I'll make sure someone comes out to get you. I imagine you'll have loads of packages."

"Hope so," Kerry answered, immediately going off into a daydream about all the things she needed for her wedding.

They were at the gate, and people were already boarding the plane.

"Have a wonderful time," Nancy said, hugging Kerry to her. "Oh, I almost forgot," she added, rummaging through her handbag. Finally she located a small white envelope and handed it to her daughter. "Here's a little something from Dad and me. Get something very special, something you've always wanted. Whether it's for the wedding or not, whatever you and Brad would like."

Tears came to Kerry's eyes as she took the envelope from her mother. She knew how tight finances were; even though both of her parents worked, there was never much extra money. It was so dear of them to do this, especially after all the expenses of the holidays. "Oh, Mom, thanks so much. But maybe it would be better if I just put it in a savings account."

"Oh, no. Absolutely not," Nancy protested. "That's just the point. Be extravagant for once in your life. You're only going to be a bride once."

Chapter 4

As soon as Kerry entered the arrivals area at the San Francisco airport, she saw her grandmother, waving frantically with a gloved hand. The sight of her immediately brought a smile to Kerry's face. She made her way through the throng of passengers and into Lisbeth's open arms.

"Oh my darling, how beautiful you look!" Lisbeth exclaimed. "My, my, an engagement does wonders for a young girl, doesn't it?" she said, gently stroking Kerry's cheek.

Kerry marveled at her grandmother's good spirits after

all she had been through recently. Charles's stroke and subsequent rehabilitation, which would never really be complete, had been devastating for her. Kerry knew her grandmother had had to summon up all her strength and courage to weather the crisis. Now, at last, she seemed to have returned to her old self.

"Thank you, Grandmother. Yes, I guess I look as good as I feel. I'm really so happy, I can't wait for Brad to come home again."

"Soon enough, he will be back, darling. In the meantime, use this time well, get yourself organized, plan the wedding. In some ways it's a blessing that he's not around all the time. You've no idea how time-consuming it is to organize a proper wedding," Lisbeth said as they exited the airport and walked toward the waiting car.

Kerry was glad to see King's familiar face behind the wheel of the car. When he spotted them, he flung the door open and ran around the car to greet them.

"Miss Kerry," he said, warmly. King was practically a member of the Morgan family. He and his wife had watched Kerry and her brother grow up, and he had always had a soft spot in his heart for Lisbeth's only granddaughter. He extended his hand politely, but Kerry opened her arms and gave him a big hug.

"How good to see you, King. I was hoping you'd be here."

"Of course, Miss Kerry," he answered, placing Kerry's small suitcase in the trunk of the car. "Why, I was nearly as excited as your grandmother when I heard you were coming. Getting married soon too, I hear. It's hard to believe, that's all I can say. When I told Mary, she was surprised too. Seems like only yesterday . . . oh, well, I'm sure you don't need to hear that from an old fellow like me."

"Not at all, King. I can hardly believe it myself," Kerry replied, sliding in beside Lisbeth in the back seat of the town car.

Lisbeth took Kerry's hand in hers and squeezed it as King skillfully navigated the car out of the airport exit and headed toward the city. It was a crystal clear day, the typical morning fog had lifted early, and both the Bay and Golden Gate bridges were visible in the distance.

"Oh, Kerry, it's so delightful to have you here. I've really been looking forward to it. It gets kind of quiet around here sometimes," she said, and Kerry detected a hint of sadness in her voice.

"I'm sure it does, Grandmother. But I'm glad to hear that Charles was able to go out at Christmas. That must have been nice."

Lisbeth looked away for a moment, and then spoke slowly. "Yes, it was good to be able to go out to the club. But of course, it wasn't the same. Never will be. Kerry, you must treasure every moment of your time with Brad. That's one hard lesson I have learned from this entire experience. You never know when your life will change forever . . ." She shook her head impatiently. "Enough of that! Now, darling," she continued, "we must make a plan so that we make the most of our time together. I'm sure you have a list a mile long. But I'm certain we'll be able to find everything you will want for the wedding in the shops here. They have such a marvelous selection."

"Anything will be better than what's available in Carson City."

"Not to worry, dear. We'll scour the shops, and what they don't have in stock we'll order for you. It's important to get exactly what you want when you're just starting out. Or as close to it as possible, anyway. Oh, it will be the most beautiful wedding ever! But you must let me know what you have in mind. I don't want my old-fashioned tastes to influence your decisions. So if I get too bossy, you just let me know," she said, patting her granddaughter's hand. "You must follow your heart and go with your own inclinations."

"Don't worry, Grandmother. I'll be happy to follow your lead anyday. You have the best sense of style of anyone I've ever known." She meant every word, as she looked over at Lisbeth in her elegant wool suit.

"Nonsense," Lisbeth insisted. "I just go with the basics, nothing too trendy or fashionable, and it seems to suit me just fine. Anyway, we'll have plenty of time to discover each other's likes and dislikes as we make our way through the weekend.

"King, you've made wonderful time. We're here already," Lisbeth announced proudly as King turned the car into the short driveway of the pristine Victorian mansion.

The house was Lisbeth's pride and joy. Built in the late

1800s and a survivor of the major San Francisco earthquake as well as all the minor ones that had followed over the years, it had been in the Morgan family for two generations. When Lisbeth had married Charles after her first husband, Kerry's grandfather, had died of a heart attack, she had lovingly restored the parts of the house that were worthy of preservation, and had renovated and modernized the kitchen and the baths to make the house more comfortable. The work she had done was an enormous success, and the house had been photographed many times for various design magazines. Each time it had been lauded as a perfect example of a Victorian home for modern times.

"You haven't been here since we rearranged the house," Lisbeth said.

"No, I haven't. Mom mentioned that you had made some changes after Charles became ill, but she wasn't quite sure what had been done."

"Well, it's quite a significant change. It's made our living area smaller, but also much more manageable. We basically cut the house in two. With Charles incapacitated and unable to take one set of stairs, let alone two, I decided that it would be so much easier if we stayed on two floors, and made the third floor a separate flat unto itself. It worked out beautifully, as most of the major rooms were able to stay exactly as we had them before. The truth is, I did it more for the company than for the financial considerations. It's so nice to know someone else is close by at night, and of course, even with the sophisticated alarm system we installed, there is still the issue of security in these big homes.

"We've been terribly lucky with the apartment—the first couple who saw the place took it right on the spot. They just moved here from Chicago, of all places. Can you imagine, already we had so much in common. They're the nicest people. They both work, and he travels like mad. Reminds me of Charles in his younger days, always on the road doing some deal or another. He works for one of the big brokerage firms down on California Street, and she's an officer at a bank. A delightful twosome. I do hope they'll stay awhile, but she's made some noises about wanting to start a family, so I think they'll be off looking for larger quarters soon. Maybe you'll have a chance to meet them while you're here. I told Chris you were coming last week.

"Anyway, enough about them. Let's get on with our day. We don't have a moment to waste." With one last squeeze of Kerry's hand, Lisbeth got out of the car and led her granddaughter into the house.

As Kerry stepped into the wide gracious hallway, she took a deep breath and all the memories of her childhood came flooding back. Lisbeth's house always smelled so delightful, a refreshing combination of the lemony scent of recently polished wood, mixed with a fragrant potpourri that she made from the dried flowers in her garden. The house was nearly exactly as she remembered it; the only major change was that many of the familiar pieces of furniture had been rearranged to accommodate the new layout.

"Your room has remained intact," Lisbeth said, as if reading her mind.

"And I've just put a fresh vase of flowers in there and

made a final check that all is in order," said the robust Mary, as she rushed down the long hallway from the kitchen to greet Kerry.

"Oh Mary, how wonderful to see you," Kerry answered in response to the warm welcome from her grandmother's longtime housekeeper and friend. They hugged, and then Kerry made her way up the elegant staircase to the room she adored.

Indeed everything was just the same as she remembered, the lovely double bed stacked high with freshly laundered antique white linens, a handknit chenille throw draped across the upholstered slipper chair, and, as Mary had promised, a vase full of colorful, fresh flowers was on the bedside table. It had been the perfect room for a little girl to dream in, and now that her dreams were coming true, it seemed only right and fitting that she should return to this special place.

"You must be starving, or thirsty at least." As Kerry unpacked her bag, which King had brought up, Lisbeth's voice came from behind her, and she turned to see her grandmother standing in the doorway. "When you've finished settling in, come back downstairs to the kitchen and Mary will fix us a little something. Oh, I'm so thrilled you're here! Why, you'd think I was the bride instead of you." Lisbeth chuckled, turning and leaving Kerry to unpack.

Kerry looked around the familiar surroundings. As always, she was drawn to the windows which faced out over the garden in the back of the house. Tie-back curtains of a soft, cheerful blue and white chintz framed the tall expanses of glass. Even now, in the middle of winter, Lisbeth was able to cultivate many beautiful plants and flowers. Her garden was the part of the house of which she was most proud, and from this enduring love of all things green had evolved a profitable and rewarding career for her grandmother.

Like some of the best things in life, it had all come about so casually, without any planning. When Lisbeth and Charles married, even though he was in his sixties and at the tail end of a magnificent and wildly successful career, he still had to travel a great deal. Lisbeth, alone and without friends in her newly adopted city, began cultivating the small patch of land at the back of the house. When Lisbeth began her experiments, she possessed only a rudimentary knowledge of plants and flowers, but she devoted herself to local horticultural methods and by the time she had finished redecorating the house and she and Charles had begun to entertain, the garden was in full bloom. In fact, it became a showcase of the property. The women in her charity groups encouraged her to help them with their own gardens. Editors at the top shelter and interior decoration magazines got wind of this new gardening wunderkind and requests to photograph the house and garden poured in. One of the more aggressive publications commissioned Lisbeth to write about her experience and from that short article came requests for more and more articles and then a column. Now her gardening column was syndicated in newspapers all across the country. Kerry knew that after Charles's stroke Lisbeth fully came to realize how important her column was to her. She'd told her that it provided a focus for her life now that her husband was incapacitated and everything she had known as routine had been turned upside down. On mornings when she was too depressed to get out of bed, thinking of poor Charles and the diminished quality of their life together, she thought of her typewriter, and of the work that was due the following week. That alone gave her the strength to throw back the covers, get out of bed, and get on with the day.

Kerry thought about that now as she surveyed the garden. It was important for a woman to maintain her independence, to have something that was hers alone, so that no matter what happened in her life she would be able to find strength and meaning in it. It was so sad that Charles had had a stroke and that her grandmother no longer had a full partner in life. The thought of anything tragic happening to Brad sent shivers down her spine. Stop it, she told herself; Brad is young and healthy. Nothing bad is going to happen to him. Banishing all dark thoughts from her mind, she turned and went downstairs to join her grandmother for lunch.

The next three days passed in a whirlwind of activity as Kerry and Lisbeth covered the entire city of San Francisco in search of all that Kerry needed for her special day.

The only time Lisbeth left Kerry was right after they arrived home each evening. She would excuse herself and go to Charles. She would sit with him in his room for an hour or so, talking to him about the day, and feeding him his dinner. Lisbeth always returned from these sessions looking a lit-

tle sad, but moments later, after she had seated herself opposite Kerry, and had recaptured her earlier focus, she once
again smiled and became her lively old self.

When Monday evening came, and they returned from
yet another arduous day of shopping, once again they found
themselves at the table, their feet sore, eager to enjoy the meal
Mary had prepared for them.

"Well, my darling, we've certainly covered some
ground. I think we've accomplished a great deal in a very
short time. Not everything, I realize, but we've got a good
head start."

Kerry beamed, recalling the generosity and kindness
Lisbeth had shown her. Each time Kerry had shown the
slightest hesitation about whether or not to buy something,
Lisbeth had jumped in, saying that a set of pots and pans, or a
complete set of everyday cutlery would be a gift from her and
Charles. Kerry was so excited about all their new acquisitions
that she had already telephoned Brad twice.

"A good start?" Kerry repeated. "Grandmother, you've
been more generous than I ever could have hoped for. I don't
know how to thank you."

"Don't be silly. There's nothing at all to do. Except
maybe to have several beautiful great-grandchildren for me
to adore and spoil, of course."

"That's a promise, but you'll have to give us a couple
of years. We've got so much to do before we get to that
stage. Brad's got to finish medical school, and I know how
much work that's going to take. I've got to finish school too,

and then start my writing career. So just be patient with us."

"Of course, my dear. The most important thing is for the two of you to take some time and enjoy each other thoroughly. Enjoy each day, and appreciate every moment you have together. Enough time for a family later. Everything changes once you have a baby. What really counts is for the two of you to be happy together. Then you can handle anything that life brings you," said Lisbeth, wiping a tear from her eye.

Lisbeth wanted to change the subject before her sadness overcame her. Knowing that tomorrow her precious granddaughter would be leaving, she gently broached the subject she had been struggling with for the past three days.

"One big piece of your wedding is still missing," she began.

"Oh, don't remind me, Grandmother." Kerry gave a discouraged sigh. "I never thought it would be so difficult to find a classic, elegant wedding gown. Everything is either too frilly or too modern. And we've looked everywhere! I don't know what I'm going to do."

"Well, I do have one last suggestion for you, and mind you, it's only that, my dear, in the strongest sense of the word."

Kerry stopped eating her salad, and looked across at Lisbeth, her expression both hopeful and confused. "What would that be?" she asked.

"Bring your tea and follow me upstairs. Mary, dinner was terrific. Now would you bring some of those cookies you baked for dessert up to my room for us?" Lisbeth asked as Kerry echoed her own thanks and they headed up the carpeted staircase.

Lisbeth directed Kerry to have a seat on her bed and then she disappeared into her dressing room, and returned only seconds later balancing a large box in her arms. "Here, let me help you," Kerry said, jumping up.

"Oh, I had forgotten how cumbersome this big box is," Lisbeth said as she struggled with it. "Let's just put it down over here." She placed the box on the floor in front of the fireplace, which had earlier been lit by Mary. It gave off just enough heat to make the room nice and cozy on a chilly night.

Ceremoniously, Lisbeth lifted the top of the box, revealing countless layers of white tissue paper. "They certainly do a good job packing, don't they? Well, I suppose some of these dresses stay in their boxes for years. I know this one has."

Kerry helped her grandmother pull away the tissue paper, and at last the contents were revealed.

"Go ahead, take it out," Lisbeth urged.

As Kerry gently lifted the gown she saw a dress more beautiful than any she had ever imagined. It was made of the softest shade of rich cream satin, the bodice was draped to fall gently around the shoulders, and the skirt was cut on the bias, giving it a fluid movement that could only have been made possible by the most skilled dressmaker. Kerry held it up to herself, matching the waistline to her own, as she turned to look at her grandmother.

"Go stand in front of the full-length mirror," Lisbeth directed, following her across the room.

"Oh, Grandmother, it's so beautiful. Where did you ever get it?"

Lisbeth smiled, thrilled to see that Kerry was so taken with the dress. "It's mine, of course, darling. I know it seems hard to believe, because it looks so up-to-date. And so small! But it is. My mother had it made for me in Paris by one of the top couturiers when I married your grandfather. My, it certainly was ages ago. I had hoped that your mother would wear it, but, as you know, she had her own ideas about weddings," she said, a bit sadly. "Well, it doesn't matter now, does it? It seems the dress might just work for you. We've skipped a generation, but that's all right. You do like it then?"

"Like it? I love it!" Kerry exclaimed. "It's really the most beautiful dress I've ever seen. And to think that I could possibly wear it . . . oh, Grandmother, thank you, thank you so much," she said, placing the dress on a chair, and rushing to hug Lisbeth.

"Well, good, dear, I'm so pleased," Lisbeth replied, returning her embrace. "Now all we have to do is see if it fits."

At that very moment, Mary entered bearing the cookies and a tea service on a silver tray.

"Ah, perfect timing, Mary. It seems we might have some alterations to do here."

Kerry had already discarded her jeans and the sweater she had been wearing. She stood naked except for a pair of skimpy bikini panties and bulky socks. Quickly she released her hair from the clip she used to pull up the front strands, and she twisted all of her long, blond hair and secured it on top of her head. Lisbeth held the dress up for her and she stepped in gingerly, silently praying that it would fit. She put her arms through the cap sleeves, and stood still as Lisbeth adjusted the back of the dress. Kerry held her breath as she felt Lisbeth begin to button the many satin-covered buttons that lined the back of the dress. Lisbeth then arranged the draped bodice and rearranged the folds of the cap sleeves around Kerry's shoulders. Mary sat on the floor and busied herself with the skirt. She ran her hands underneath the lovely fabric, fluffing and straightening out the generous layers of cream satin.

"Okay, you can exhale now," Lisbeth advised her. She stood back, assessing her beautiful granddaughter. "Well, if we had flown to Paris and gone to the couturier ourselves, and then sat through countless fittings, we couldn't have done much better," she declared.

"With a pair of modest heels, I don't think we'll even need to shorten it," Mary added, sitting back on her legs and looking admiringly at Kerry. "You don't need to worry about being taller than Brad, do you?" Mary asked. "I hear that he's a tall, handsome young man," she added.

"Oh, he certainly is," Kerry replied, so pleased with the way she looked in the dress. "No matter how high a heel I wear, I'll never be taller than he is," she answered. "And he is handsome, and wonderful, and I'm really the luckiest girl in the world!" she exclaimed, turning to face her grandmother. Now she saw tears of happiness in Lisbeth's eyes.

"Oh, dear, I'm so pleased. You'll be the most beautiful

bride. Now let's get you out of it. I'll have it professionally cleaned and pressed and I'll send it off to you in Carson City."

Before Kerry took off the gown she walked over to the full-length mirror. She looked like a fairy-tale princess. With a dreamy smile on her face, she imagined walking down the aisle holding her father's arm. And there, at the altar, Brad would be waiting for her, to take her as his wife. Blessed by family and friends, they would go off arm in arm to start their new life together.

PART
II

Chapter 5

It was sometime late in March when the bubble burst. The uneasy feeling first hit Kerry as she was driving home from Cutler's one night. Her eyes began to blur, her head pounded. Blinking against the oncoming headlights, she steadied herself and was somehow able to get safely home. But the next night on her way home from work a wave of nausea swept over her so quickly that she was forced to pull over to the side of the road. Panicked and perspiring heavily despite the cold, she sat clutching the steering wheel. She hadn't eaten much that day, she had been so busy studying for exams. Maybe it was just low blood sugar that was causing her to feel weak and so terribly sick. Maybe it was that nasty flu everyone seemed to have. She waited for what seemed like hours by the side of the freeway, until she finally felt well enough to continue.

Once safely inside the kitchen, she scrounged around for something to calm her stomach. Sitting at the breakfast table eating some saltines, she was overcome with a fear greater than any she had previously known. Kerry had experienced a bad bout of flu before, but this was a different feeling altogether. She hadn't eaten anything so it wasn't food poisoning. She racked her brain, trying to recall when she had last had her period. She remembered the one before Christmas, as she had been grateful that it had come and gone before Brad arrived. From then on she couldn't remember having had one. She had never been the least bit regular, but surely she must have had another since December. In all the excitement and anxiety about planning the wedding, she simply must have forgotten the exact date. Oh no, it just wasn't possible, it would be the worst thing in the world that could happen. No, she screamed over and over in her mind.

After taking a hot bath she lay down, but sleep would not come, and by the time the hands on her little clock showed three A.M., Kerry was one hundred percent certain that she was indeed pregnant. All she needed to confirm this was a simple test like the ones available at any pharmacy. The only problem was she couldn't possibly buy one of those kits at the drugstore in Carson City. Gossipy old Mrs. Childs would surely notice her purchase and word of Coach Will's daughter having bought a home pregnancy test kit would be all around the small town long before she was even able to open the box.

So well before first light, Kerry was up and dressed and on her way to Reno to find a store where she wouldn't be recognized. After purchasing the kit she drove to school. Even though she knew she wouldn't be able to concentrate very well, she didn't want to miss a class with exams only two weeks away. Clutching the small paper bag that contained the box that could possibly change her future, she walked to her classroom, but as she neared it, she took the hallway to the left and headed for the bathroom at the end of the corridor. Alone in the cramped stall, surrounded by cold industrial metal and harsh fluorescent light, she watched as a clear blue line appeared down the center of the test paper she dipped in the small vial containing her urine. Kerry watched in wide-eyed horror as the line turned a deeper shade of blue as if to leave no question as to the outcome of the test. She frantically applied more urine to the paper, and once again watched as the blue lines appeared. Her eyes clenched shut, she prayed it wasn't true. The harsh green metal of the stall seemed to close in on her, and she felt the need to escape.

She ran back down the hallway and out through the glass doors toward the parking lot. She was still holding the wet blue paper tightly in her fist.

Kerry drove aimlessly, not paying much attention to passing cars, warning signs, or traffic lights. She was well out of town before she was aware that she was headed toward Tahoe, to a remote place which she and Brad had claimed as their own several years before. Kerry saw the skiers gliding down the mountainside on the slope across the lake, but all she could think of was Brad and their Christmas holiday. They made love often and with the passion of two people deeply in love, but they had also been very careful always to prevent that love from creating a child they weren't yet ready for. Kerry closed her eyes and tried to recall a time when they had been careless, swept away by their desire and had thrown caution to the wind. But she knew that every single time Brad had been prepared. So it must have been one of those cruel, rare accidents that could happen to anyone. But why had it happened to them, she cried inwardly. Two young people with such hopes and dreams, two who were doing everything in their power to start their new life together on the right track, planning and taking responsibility for their future. Suddenly Kerry felt the full force of the cold afternoon air coming through her open car window. She realized it was getting late and she was due at the restaurant. She drove back toward town.

Kerry served her tables with all the efficiency and charm of a robot. She walked as if in a trance through the kitchen to pick up her orders, then back out through the dining room to deliver them to the waiting customers. When the restaurant had cleared out and they began cleaning up for the evening, the waitress who worked the section of the dining room next to Kerry's came over to her.

"Boy, you look like you had a rough day. I was worried about you all night. It was just too busy to stop and see if you were all right. What's the matter?"

Unable to face the news herself, let alone share it with a woman she hardly knew, Kerry tried her best to be polite.

"Thanks, Suzy. You're right, I did have a tough day, but I'll be fine." Even as she said the words she knew that it would be a long while before she was fine, and tears filled her eyes uncontrollably.

Suzy put her tray down and rushed to Kerry's side.

"Oh dear," she said. "Oh, honey, I didn't mean to upset you even more. I was just so worried about you. We always expect a big smile from you, you're always so cheerful, and tonight you just weren't yourself."

Suzy put her arms around Kerry, who welcomed her embrace. "Oh, Suzy, thank you for being so nice," she sobbed. "I'll be all right. I . . . I . . . just can't talk about it now."

"That's all right," Suzy said, rubbing her back and trying to calm her. "When you can, and if you need a friend, you just let me know. Remember that nothing's ever as bad as it seems at first."

Suzy's kindness made Kerry sob all the harder, but when she heard someone else swing open the kitchen door, she pulled back and began once again to clean the tables.

"Don't be silly, girl," Suzy said, taking the cloth from her hands. "You go on and get out of here. You could use a good night's sleep. I'll finish up for you."

Kerry began to protest, but Suzy shooed her away. Kerry thanked her, hurriedly put her coat on, and left the restaurant.

Thankful that no one was up when she reached home, Kerry went straight to her room and prepared for bed. Still feeling slightly nauseated, she lay in bed with her hands clutched over her belly, which in no time would begin to grow and change to accommodate the unborn child inside. She prayed for the strength to deal with this unexpected turn of events. No matter how hard she tried to visualize herself in her bridal gown walking down the aisle toward Brad, all she could see each time she dared to close her eyes was a deep blue line piercing a stark white background.

Chapter 6

For the next few days, Kerry tried to adjust to the fact that she was pregnant. She longed to share the news with Brad so that together they could plan how to handle the situation, but each time she spoke with him he seemed to be under such pressure about his exams that she hadn't been able to summon up the courage to tell him. It wasn't really something she wanted to discuss with him on the telephone; she wanted him to be by her side when she told him the news. She considered flying down to Los Angeles, but she would have to explain that to her parents, which might prove to be even more difficult than waiting another two weeks for him to come home. So she guarded her secret, and waited.

Strangely, life went on as usual, classes went on as scheduled, there was always a pile of work waiting for her at the insurance agency, and a crowd of diners to serve at Cutler's. Willy and Coach left each morning, talking about the next football game, and her mother went off to work at the inn.

But Kerry had changed dramatically since the morning she'd bought the pregnancy kit. She was no longer a carefree bride-to-be with all her hopes and dreams ahead of her, but rather a confused, frightened young woman faced with the prospect of becoming a mother in only six months.

Kerry told herself that as soon as Brad came home

everything would be all right. They had always vowed that whatever happened to them they would be able to handle it as long as they were honest and open with each other.

But that vow would soon be put to the test, as they faced the biggest crisis of their young lives, Kerry thought, as she slowly made her way through the stack of claims on her desk. She had just finished a long drawn-out conversation with an irate customer when the phone rang.

"Yes, Kerry McKinney speaking, how may I help you?" She caught herself just in time from sounding irritated rather than helpful and cheery as a customer service representative was supposed to be.

"You sound a little harassed, Ms. McKinney, what's the problem?" came the familiar voice.

Kerry's anxieties and fears suddenly melted away when she heard Brad's voice. "Hi, you. Are you here already?" she asked, hopefully. If that was the case, she would call in sick to Cutler's and go off to meet him as soon as possible.

"We have arrived," he answered. "We were able to get organized and leave L.A. around four this morning, and we made good time, so we thought we'd head straight up to Kirkwood and get in some afternoon skiing, then I'll be back in time to pick you up at the restaurant tonight."

Hearing that he was already in Carson City and that he wasn't coming right over to see her suddenly incensed Kerry. How could he be so cavalier, so uncaring? Then she realized that he couldn't possibly know the pain she was suffering since she had chosen to keep the secret to herself, not wanting to upset him before his exams. But now none of that seemed to matter; all she cared about was being able to be with Brad and tell him about her pregnancy. She was impatient, angry, and tired of carrying the enormous burden all by herself.

"Kerry, are you there? Listen, I've got to run, or we won't have any time at all. They're predicting some snow late this afternoon. But who knows, maybe it will hold off, they're usually wrong. I'll see you tonight, okay? I'll pick you up at Cutler's."

Kerry bit her bottom lip, trying to contain the tears that were already filling her eyes.

"Kerry, what's the matter? Is something wrong?"

Something wrong? she wanted to cry out. Their entire world had changed in the last couple of weeks! She breathed deeply, trying to control her emotions, knowing that falling apart now would only make matters worse.

"No, no I'm just anxious to see you, that's all. I miss you. And I have so much to tell you."

"I know, angel, and we'll be together in only a few hours. Now calm down. You sound like you're really under a lot of pressure. I'll make everything better tonight, I promise. I'm just going to ski with George and Jeff for a few hours, and then I'll come and get you."

Kerry looked up to see her supervisor, Miss Kenton, headed her way and decided that she had better get off the phone.

"Okay, but be careful if it starts to snow."

"Look out your window—it's perfectly clear. We'll be fine. Bye now. See you tonight."

She hung up without even saying good-bye and quickly helped Miss Kenton search for a lost claim.

Chapter 7

Nancy McKinney rushed around the lodge's spacious kitchen, hastily arranging an odd assortment of cookies and pastries on the last platter she had been able to locate. Once the storm had hit, all the guests had come in from the slopes. Most of them were now scattered about the living room and library, and they all wanted tea, or drinks, or something to eat.

The Twin Pines Inn was normally a quiet, relaxed place. It attracted serious skiers who checked in, left just after daybreak for the slopes, and returned for an early dinner, after which they were ready to turn in. It was unusual for them to have more than a dozen guests during the late afternoon, but now, Nancy estimated, they had at least forty. The staff was not prepared to handle that number of people. Luckily, Nancy thought as she heard a roar of laughter from a group gathered in front of the enormous stone fireplace, everyone was in good spirits, glad to be inside the warm, cozy lodge and out of the wind and blinding snow.

The noise level at the inn was so high that it was a few moments before the desperate cries of a woman could be heard.

"Please, someone, help," she cried, waving her arms about frantically, trying to get someone's attention. "I need help now," she screamed.

Nancy saw the woman and rushed to her side.

"Come quickly, please, someone call for help, call an ambulance, and the police!" she cried breathlessly.

"All right, all right, someone will call, just try to calm down and we'll help. Tell us what happened," Nancy urged, holding the woman's hands in her own.

"Call the police, Don, right now," Nancy yelled out to one of the busboys. "Go in the back and tell them we also need medical help, and an ambulance."

"Oh, it was horrible," the woman said. Nancy could feel her hands trembling uncontrollably as she held them. "My husband and I were on our way back to our cabin, and as we were walking we heard this loud noise, the sound of tires screeching and then a big crash. We walked out toward the road, and there . . . oh . . . it's awful. It's a terrible accident. The little car didn't have a chance against the big truck. You can't see a thing out there, it's a total white-out—they must not have seen it coming at all. My husband told me to come back here, and he went to see if he could help. He's still out there. Please, someone, call an ambulance. Now."

"We've already done that," Nancy assured the woman, who was clearly in shock.

The crowd's attention had turned to the woman, and silence filled the room. For a few moments it seemed that no one knew what to do, then common sense took over and the guests snapped into action. Men set down their drinks and began pulling on their boots, while several of the women scrambled to get blankets and other equipment they felt might be useful.

Nancy had taken over the responsibility for calling the police. She clutched the phone to her ear and listened as the operator assured her that an ambulance had already been dispatched.

"We've already had two reports about that accident," the operator said. "Sounds like a nasty one, I've got men on the way, but the roads aren't any clearer down here try to do what you can for them, and call me back with a report."

Nancy rushed back to her own office, grabbed her coat and hat. She too joined the line of guests as they marched out the front door and forged a trail down the long drive that led to the highway.

The first men reached the end of the path and began assessing the situation. By the time Nancy could make out the silhouette of the huge truck, upended and turned on its side, the would-be rescuers were already hacking away at the metal door, trying to free the driver. Sirens sounded vaguely in the distance.

Nancy stood frozen, her eyes focused on the small car

that was nearly indistinguishable under a blanket of newly fallen snow. Somehow she had known, from the very first moment she saw the panicked woman waving her arms about, that something terrible had happened that would directly involve her own life,

Brad, thoughtful as always, had called to tell her that he would be delayed dropping his roommates off at the inn. They had been caught on the mountain and had had to wait for the rescue crew to go up and get them down. He assured her they could make it, it just might take them a little longer than usual, and he didn't want her to worry.

"I know these roads like the back of my proverbial hand," he'd assured her. "I remember driving on Dad's lap when I was not more than four or five. Don't worry, I'll take it slow. As long as I don't miss the turn, we should be there by four."

Still, Nancy had cautioned him over and over again to drive carefully. She'd assured him that she would wait for him, and that, if necessary, they could leave the little Volkswagen at the inn and take the four-wheel-drive vehicle down to pick up Kerry.

"We may just need to do that, the little Bug's greatest act is not in blizzards," Brad had said.

Now as she stood staring in horror at the crushed mound of metal, she recalled that conversation and heard Brad's laughter ringing in her ears. "Don't worry, I'll be there. Nothing can happen to me. I have to take care of your daughter, remember? She would never forgive me if I had an accident."

She forced herself to move in the direction of the car, where a group of men were still trying to determine what they should do until the professionals arrived. They knelt down around the car, beside the accumulation of snow, with their hands trying desperately to look inside the crushed vehicle.

The sound of sirens grew louder, and with the arrival of the medical crew things seemed to Nancy to move very quickly. She watched as they used torches to cut apart the remains of the car and then pulled three motionless bodies from the wreckage. Her entire body was shaking. She was told that all three were still breathing. She rushed forward to try to get a closer look at Brad, but was stopped by a policeman.

"Ma'am, you'll have to stand back," he cautioned her, holding out his gloved hands to block her path.

"But that's Brad," she screamed. "I want to see if he's going to be all right. I want to tell him I'm here."

"Not now, ma'am. They're going to take him to the hospital. That's where he belongs if he's going to have a chance at all. Now, please, move back and clear the way so they can put them in the ambulance."

They loaded the three stretchers and slammed the back door of the ambulance shut. As suddenly as they had appeared, the rescuers disappeared into the thick white darkness.

Trudging at full speed, Nancy made her way back to the lodge and telephoned Coach at school.

"Will, it's awful," she cried, falling apart as soon as he came to the phone. She tried to get control of herself, and as calmly as she could, she relayed the news of the accident to him.

"I'm going to go find Jim, and tell him. Then we can swing by and pick up Sara and Amy. By that time they should have already admitted them to the hospital. I'll meet you there."

Coach was the first person Nancy saw when she entered the hospital. He rushed to her side, and before she could speak he put his arms around her and hugged her tightly.

Pulling back from him, she looked at his face and saw only profound worry. "The boys are all being taken care of," he began. "George and Jeff seem to have come through pretty well. George got off easy, he's just very shaken up. Jeff's arm is broken, but they've already set it. If all goes well, they might be released as early as tomorrow."

Nancy's anxiety mounted. "And Brad? What about Brad?"

"Brad's in very bad shape, Nancy. He suffered the most trauma in the crash. He was barely conscious when they brought him in, and right after they thought they had him stabilized, he went into a coma." He stopped and took a deep breath, and for only the second time in their twenty-three-year marriage, she saw tears in his eyes. "The doctors aren't promising that he'll make it through the night."

"Oh, Will," she cried, and collapsed into her husband's arms. What she had most dreaded was coming true, and she ached with fear for Kerry and Brad, and for all those who loved him so. Fighting to regain her senses, she looked around and asked, "Where is everyone?"

"I went to pick Jim up at the office, but Sara and Amy are out shopping. We haven't been able to locate them yet. Jim is in with Brad now, but he can only stay for a minute. I waited until you got here, but now I had better go get Kerry. I don't think we should just call her. I don't want her on the roads by herself."

"Not after hearing about the accident, no, you're right. Why don't you go on now. I'll go down and wait until Jim comes out."

"All right," he sighed, knowing how difficult the task ahead of him was going to be. Thinking about it on the way to Cutler's, Coach could not recall anything in his life that he had dreaded as much as he did telling Kerry about the accident.

Chapter 8

Kerry finished setting the tables at her station. Because of the weather, they would be unusually busy tonight. Cut-

ler's location right in the center of town made it easy to get
to, even in the worst weather. And certainly this was the worst
weather Kerry could remember. While driving from school
to the restaurant through the blinding snow, she'd thought
about Brad and his friends, and hoped they hadn't gotten
stuck up on the mountain. Ever since she had hung up the
phone with him, Kerry had felt guilty about being so upset
with him. His decision to go skiing made perfect sense. It was
just that she was so anxious to see him and to tell him that
they were going to have a baby. Kerry comforted herself with
the fact that in only a few more hours she would be in his
arms again, and everything would fall into place.

Within the hour Kerry no longer had a minute to herself. The restaurant filled up, and they were short of help since
one of the waitresses hadn't been able to get her car out of her
snowy driveway. Kerry worked at double speed, helping out
as best she could at the abandoned group of tables, while at
the same time trying to give her own group the attention and
service they deserved. She heard the bell that signaled that
another of her orders was ready, and was just on her way back
to the kitchen when she saw Coach enter the restaurant.

The McKinneys were longtime regulars at Cutler's, but
never had she seen Coach come into the restaurant by himself.

At first she thought that he too may have been trapped
by the weather and had come in with a friend for a quick
drink. But then she read the look on his face as he frantically
searched the restaurant for her. In the split second when his
eyes met hers, Kerry knew that something was horribly

wrong. A thousand thoughts raced through her mind in that moment, but for some reason she settled on her mother. Something must have happened up at the inn, and now her father was coming to tell her. But why wouldn't they send Willy, or Brad, to get her, so that Coach could stay with Nancy? She rushed toward the front of the restaurant to her father.

"Dad, what are you doing here?" she said as she approached, wiping her hands on her apron and trying to remain calm.

Coach looked at his daughter for a long moment, then put his arms around her. This rare display of affection only upset Kerry more. She pulled back and looked at him.

"Dad, what are you doing here? Something is wrong, isn't it? I just know it. What's the matter?"

"Kerry," he began slowly. "Kerry, honey, there's been an accident."

"An accident, oh no. What's happened? Is Mom hurt?"

"It's not Mom, honey," he said. "I'm afraid it's Brad, Kerry. He's been very badly hurt. I want to hurry and get you to the hospital in case he regains consciousness."

"Did he have an accident on the slopes?"

"No, honey, a car accident on the way up to the inn. But please, let's just tell Mr. Cutler that you have an emergency and that you have to leave. I'll pick you up out front."

"Okay, I'll be right out," she said, the shock beginning to flow through her entire body. She ran past her tables at full speed, frantically searching for Mr. Cutler.

• • •

Kerry forced herself to keep up with her father's long strides as they made their way down the long corridor toward the intensive care unit. Never had she been so overcome with despair as she was when she saw all the people who were dearest to her gathered at the end of the hallway. They spoke in whispers.

She was not allowed to see Brad; the doctors forbade anyone to disrupt their lifesaving efforts. She sat silently throughout the night on the hard wooden bench outside his room, her mother on one side, Sara Evans on the other. At one point, two weary-looking policemen approached Brad's father and introduced themselves as the officers who had investigated the collision. They said they'd determined that it had been an accident in the truest sense of the word. The driver of the truck was not at fault; the weather was. Brad had turned in front of the truck. Apparently, he hadn't seen it coming.

The following morning, Coach took charge and insisted that they take turns returning home for a shower and something to eat. Kerry adamantly refused, and her father finally gave up trying to change her mind.

Kerry sat with her hands folded across her stomach, protecting the unborn child of the man she loved, a man who might not live through another night. She was torn between running into her mother's arms and revealing her secret, or shouting at her to leave her alone. She was so tired of hearing everyone telling her what to do. The only words she wanted to hear were from Brad's doctors. She wanted them to come out from behind the forbidding metal doors and tell her that he was going to be all right. That he would hold her in his arms so that she could tell him how much she loved him. But as she sat for hours staring at the doors, the only people who crossed the threshold were grim-faced doctors and nurses.

Sometimes, to break the monotony, they would move to a small waiting room down the hall where a television played continuously. Usually they were alone in the room, so when a stranger entered late in the afternoon, they all turned to look at him.

The man looked like he was in his late twenties. He wore an old tweed jacket over an ill-fitting white shirt, and his awkwardly knotted necktie indicated that he was not used to wearing one. How sad, Kerry thought as she watched him enter the room. Someone in his family must be very ill, and he's made an effort to look nice for them. He looked scared, and very uncomfortable, and she felt sorry for him. She'd already turned her attention back to the *People* magazine she had been reading when she heard him speak.

"Mrs. Evans?" he asked, hesitantly.

Sara and Jim looked up at him, and Jim reached over and took Sara's hand protectively in his.

"Yes," Brad's mother said slowly. "I'm Sara Evans."

The young man put his hands in his pockets, and walked toward them. "Mrs. Evans, and Mr. Evans?"

"Yes, I'm Jim Evans. What can we do for you?"

"I'm Noland Rogers," he began, and sensing that his name meant nothing to either of them, he continued. "I'm the one who was driving the truck. The truck that hit your son." His face was pained, and for a moment Kerry continued to feel sorry for him.

"You . . ." Jim Evans began, "you were driving?"

"Yes, sir, I was. And I wanted to come here and tell you how sorry I am for what happened. I've been drivin' the rig for nearly ten years, and nothing like this has ever happened before. I drive for my dad. We live over in Truckee. I . . . I was just trying to get back over to Carson City for the night, put the truck away out of the terrible weather. I was going as slowly as I could. I really didn't see your boy's car until it was too late. There was nothing I could do. I . . . I just wanted to come and say that I hope he's better very soon."

When Jim finally spoke, his voice was tense, as if he could barely control his anger.

"We don't know yet how Brad is going to do. If he's even going to live. The doctors don't really know for certain. My wife and I, and Brad's wife-to-be over there," he said, pointing to Kerry, who also just continued to stare at the young man, "we're here praying for him. That's about all we can do for the time being. But, thank you for coming. We thank you," he finished, looking away from the young man.

The truck driver turned to look at Kerry, and when their eyes locked she was unable to hold back what she had been thinking ever since the man had identified himself to Jim and Sara.

"You!" she screamed. "You are the one who caused this to happen! Do you know how badly injured Brad is? The doctors say he might not live through another night. They won't even let me see him. He's in a coma. Do you realize what you've done to all of us. You're a monster!" she screamed. "You should be locked up forever, and still that wouldn't be enough punishment for you," she said, as Jim rushed to her side and tried to calm her.

"Kerry, Kerry, you mustn't get so upset. It won't help anything. Please." He held her against him as she collapsed into uncontrollable sobs.

"I think you had better go now," Jim told the young man.

"I'm sorry," he repeated brokenly before he backed out of the room.

Kerry's outburst brought a new wave of tears to Brad's mother. Jim moved to comfort her and Kerry left the room, hoping that a walk around the corridors would help her calm down.

Coach came later in the day, bringing Amy, and then driving Sara back home. Jim stayed at the hospital, but by the end of the evening there was no change at all in Brad's prognosis. Kerry spent another long night curled up in one of the chairs in the waiting room.

Brad died the following day. By chance, Sara had been allowed to see him only moments before. The doctors had made their morning rounds, and had indicated that she could go and sit by his bed for a few minutes. Kerry took the opportunity to go down to the cafeteria.

When she rounded the corner carrying the cardboard box filled with cups of coffee for everyone, she knew immediately that the worst had happened. At the end of the hall she saw Sara Evans, sitting on a wooden chair, her body bent over, her head in her hands. Jim and Amy stood next to her, looking helpless. Kerry threw the box down on the nurses' station, and ran down the corridor. She knelt next to Sara and they held each other tightly.

"Oh, Kerry, why . . . why did it have to happen? Why Brad?" Sara sobbed.

"I don't know, I don't know," Kerry cried into her shoulder as they held on to one another.

Sara pulled back from her. "There's something you have to know," she began. "Right before . . . right before he died he was alert for a moment. He called out your name."

This news struck Kerry like a physical assault. She stared at Sara, and then suddenly became light-headed. Fearing she would faint, she reached out to Brad's father. Jim and Amy led her over to the other chair where she sat for what seemed like hours. It was alarmingly still in the hallways as the nurses went in and out of the room where the man she loved had just died.

Nancy and Coach came as soon as they heard. Despite his own grief, Coach tried once again to organize the others. Soon it was clear that the only thing to do was go home and begin making the necessary arrangements from there. Coach led Kerry down the long, bleak hallway. Once again she thought she was going to pass out. Leaning against her father, she silently prayed that she would awaken from this nightmare.

Chapter 9

A week after they buried Brad, Kerry slowly came to the realization that no amount of crying would lessen her grief, and that there was nothing she or anyone else could do to return her life to the way it had been just a short time ago. Still she ached, and she longed for some explanation to ease the profoundness of her pain. Never had she dealt with emotions that were so deep, so raw, or with a loss that was truly irreversible. The man she loved was gone from her life forever.

She was also in the fourth month of pregnancy. Even though she had no appetite and barely ate, each day her clothes felt a little tighter. She had not yet seen a doctor since she'd discovered that she was carrying Brad's child, and she knew it was long overdue, both for her sake and especially the baby's. Still, she couldn't go to her regular doctor, and if she went to anyone else in the area, her parents would find out about it in no time. She set herself a deadline of one week to make a plan for her future, which was now so very different from what she had hoped it would be.

At the end of the week, she was still unable to make any decisions. She went through the days as if on automatic pilot, and although her schedule was finally back to normal, she continued to feel like a total stranger in her own world.

Kerry could not even begin to imagine telling her mother that she was pregnant. She would be shocked and angry and would immediately tell Coach, whose reaction Kerry was not prepared to face. Her father had not been the same since the day of Brad's funeral, and she feared the knowledge of her pregnancy would push him even further into a depression, or worse yet, into a rage. Kerry loved her parents and she knew they loved her, but they were very strict, conservative people who expected her and her brother to conform to their beliefs and values. They would view her condition as shameful, and as bringing shame upon the entire family. The last thing she wanted to do was hurt and disappoint her parents.

Kerry knew she needed someone who could sit down with her and discuss her situation calmly and sensibly, weigh her options, and help her decide on the best course of action to take. Unfortunately, while she knew a couple of her close friends would sympathize with her, none of them would know what to do for her.

From a phone booth at the university, Kerry called the only person with whom she felt she could share her secret. Sitting in the tiny booth with the glass door pulled shut, she took a deep breath as she dialed, knowing that the conversation could go in one of two directions—either she would get the help she needed on her terms, or by tomorrow at this time she would be facing her parents. Faith in her own instincts, coupled with a feeling deep in her heart that she was doing the right thing, made her able to complete the call. Still, her fingers were shaking, and she suddenly felt that she couldn't breathe. She pushed open the door of the booth and waited for her call to go through.

Chapter 10

This time when Kerry arrived in San Francisco, only King was there to greet her.

"Your grandmother says to tell you how sorry she is," he said, coming forward to take her luggage from her. "She had to take Charles to the doctor, and this was the only time he could see him. I left her at the doctor's office with Mary, and I'll go back for them after I drop you off at the house.

"What's the matter, Miss Kerry? You look so sad. Don't be troubled, I'll be back with them in no time."

"Oh, I'm all right, King," Kerry insisted, trying to put

on a cheerful face. But the truth was she was disappointed, terribly disappointed. Somehow she'd expected to get off the plane in California, and run directly into the arms of her grandmother, who would take care of everything and solve all her problems. The realization that there were other things going on in her grandmother's life, and that she couldn't just drop everything and be there for her, struck Kerry like a sharp blow to the stomach. The harsh reality of her situation sank in at once. She was a big girl now, with a big-girl problem, and even though she was lucky to have someone who was willing to help her, she was going to have to start to help herself.

All alone in the big house, Kerry made her way up to her room. Everything was just as she had left it two months ago, except that now the colors of the fresh flowers didn't look so vibrant, and the beautiful room didn't seem nearly as cozy and inviting. Kerry knew it was her dramatically changed state of mind which made everything look different. Before, her world had been filled with promise and hope, whereas now it was colored by shadows and despair.

"Kerry, where are you, dear?" Lisbeth's voice called out. "I'm so sorry I couldn't come out to meet you," she said, mounting the stairs.

Kerry roused herself and went out into the hallway. "Yes, I'm here," she replied. "Don't worry about not coming for me. King was right there at the gate. Is Charles okay?"

"Yes, yes, he's fine, dear. A little tired from the excursion, but the doctor gave him a new medication that's supposed to eliminate the problems he's recently developed."

Lisbeth hugged her, then pulled away and looked at her. "You look well, darling, but a little tired. I wouldn't expect anything else after all you've been through these last weeks. Oh, my dear, I can't imagine how hard it's been for you, and for everyone who was close to Brad. How's his family holding up?"

"His father seems to have buried himself in his work, and in time his sister, Amy, will be fine, I think. I'm worried about Sara, his mother, though. She seems to have taken it the hardest. She's very depressed and refuses to speak to anyone aside from Mr. Evans and Amy."

"It's been said for ages that one of the most painful things in life is to bury one of your children, and I am sure that it is true. People express their grief in different ways. It might just take Mrs. Evans a little longer than the rest of her family to recover. No, recover is the wrong word, really. None of you will ever fully recover from this loss. You will just learn to live with it, and to accept it on some level. No matter how long you live, there will always be a part of your heart that belongs to Brad. Even after you've found a new love, married, and started a new life, Brad will oftentimes be in your thoughts. It's only right and natural to feel that way after we've loved someone so deeply.

"But we don't need to talk about that right now," she said, squeezing Kerry's hands. "I'm sure you must be hungry. Mary was up early this morning making your favorite meal. In spite of all the extra hours she's been putting in with Charles, she still had the strength to shop and prepare everything. I truly don't know where she gets her energy, it seems boundless. There have been days recently when I wished she could transfer some of it to me."

"No doubt you could have used it—sounds like you've been having a rough time," Kerry said.

"It will pass, I have been assured," Lisbeth responded. "I guess it's been a tough time for all of us. I must tell you I was very worried about you after our conversation the other day. I'm anxious to hear what this is all about. Let's have dinner first and then we can sit quietly and talk. How's that sound?"

Kerry felt the comforting touch of Lisbeth's arm around her shoulder as they went downstairs for dinner.

King and Mary joined them at the table, since they had agreed to stay on that night to attend to Charles. The conversation was light and Kerry even managed an occasional smile and to act interested in the topics they discussed. Even though Mary's specially prepared pot roast with vegetables and new potatoes was Kerry's favorite, her appetite was not up to it, and she moved the food around her plate like a small child who was trying to avoid eating greens. Toward the end of the meal she began to feel fearful and uncertain because the time was at hand to tell her grandmother the truth about her situation.

As she had expected, Lisbeth suggested that the two of them take their dessert and tea in the living room, where they could be alone and get to the heart of the problem that had brought Kerry to San Francisco.

Kerry took one of the big upholstered chairs next to

the fireplace, and Lisbeth settled into the settee facing it. The fire burned softly and gave a warm glow to the room. Even so, Kerry wrapped her arms around herself, trying to fend off the chills and the uncontrollable shaking of her entire body.

"Darling, whatever is it? You look as if you're about to be ill, and you hardly touched your dinner. What's the matter, dear?"

Kerry looked across at her grandmother, and then lowered her eyes. "I'm going to have a baby."

"Oh, my . . . oh my."

Now that Kerry finally had told someone her secret, she suddenly felt a sense of release. She wanted so badly to go to her grandmother, to bury her head in her ample bosom, and to hear her words of comfort telling her that everything was going to be all right, but she was still uncertain of her grandmother's reaction.

"Oh, Kerry, I'm . . . I suppose I'm sorry to learn this. I . . . I just don't quite know what to say. Can you tell me anything more about it? When did this happen? And how long have you known?"

Kerry raised her eyes to her grandmother. "Oh, Grandmother, please don't be angry with me. Ever since I found out, I've been so afraid that everyone would be mad. It was an accident, a terrible twist of fate, just like the accident that killed Brad. Don't you see, I never meant for this to happen. We had our whole lives to look forward to. I've been so frightened, ever since I found out, that I haven't been able to share this secret with anyone. You're the first person I've told."

Lisbeth stared back at her. "What do you mean, darling? Surely you must have told Brad right away."

Kerry steeled herself to hold back her tears. She had to tell Lisbeth everything, so that she would understand.

"No, Grandmother, Brad never knew. I found out I was pregnant only a couple of weeks before he was due to come home. He was in the middle of studying for his exams, and he sounded like he was under so much pressure. I decided to wait and tell him, in person, the minute he came home." Kerry paused and quickly caught her breath. "When he finally did get to Carson City, he was with his roommates, and he called me at work to tell me that they were going skiing for the day, and that, later that night, he would pick me up from Cutler's. I was upset, but couldn't explain why, because I was at work. It was silly of me to be angry since I couldn't leave the office anyway. Still, I was a little sharp with him, I know. I told him to go ahead and go skiing with his friends, and that I would see him later as we had planned. That was the last time I ever spoke to him."

"Oh, dear, how tragic," Lisbeth said. "You were never even able to tell him. And now he's gone."

At those words Kerry couldn't help herself. She ran to her grandmother's open arms. Her body shook with sobs as she let out all the emotions that had been pent up for weeks.

Kerry's sobs eventually subsided, and she pulled away from her grandmother. "Grandmother, I'm so sorry to bring my problem to you, but you are the only one who I knew would understand, and would help me. I wanted to tell Mom and Dad, but I thought it would be best if Brad and I did it together. But we never had the chance. And ever since Brad died, Dad has been so withdrawn and quiet, I just couldn't bring myself to tell him and Mom all alone."

"Oh dear, how hard all of this must be for you. You were right to call me, Kerry, and I'll help you in any way I can. Now, when is the baby due?"

"I think around the end of September, but I could be off by a week or two."

"Well, what did the doctor say? He should be able to tell you within a few days, even though first babies are fairly unpredictable."

"I . . . I haven't been to a doctor."

"You haven't seen a doctor?" Lisbeth asked, unable to disguise the shock in her voice. "What do you mean, dear? How are you certain that you're even pregnant, without having a confirmation from an expert?"

"Believe me, Grandmother, I couldn't be more certain. But you know what a small, gossipy place Carson City is. Mom and Dad know everyone. If I went to see my doctor, the news would be all over town before I was even able to throw away that paper gown they give you."

"Kerry, this is nothing to joke about. Of all the things you've told me this evening, I must tell you that I find this the most shocking. You have an obligation to yourself, and to your unborn child, to be examined by a doctor. The first several months of pregnancy are crucial for both the mother and the child, and you've already passed into the second trimester without seeing anyone. Oh, Kerry, I wish you had come ear-lier."

Lisbeth's lecture brought fresh tears to Kerry's eyes. Everything her grandmother had said Kerry had already said to herself a thousand times.

"Oh, darling, please don't cry. I don't mean to be harsh with you, but it is so important that you have the best care available. Tomorrow morning, first thing, we will find you a doctor, and make an appointment. Once we've done that we can sit down and consider your options. Then we can decide how we are going to tell your parents. In the meantime let's both try to get a good night's sleep. I must admit, I'm ex-hausted. It's been quite a day."

"Me too, Grandmother," Kerry agreed as the two women walked up the stairs with their arms wrapped about each other's waist.

At the entrance to Kerry's room, Lisbeth stopped and took her granddaughter's face in her hands. "Get some rest, dear. Now that I know what the problem is, we will handle it together, in the best way we can. Sleep well, my dear."

Kerry returned her kiss on the cheek, and then softly shut the door behind her. She was truly blessed to have Lis-beth in her life. Still, she knew that by no means were her troubles over. The toughest days and the hardest decisions still lay ahead.

PART

III

PART

Chapter 11

Chris Brooks carefully guided the Volvo wagon into the very tight parking area. The width of the space at the end of the big house's driveway had certainly not been designed to accommodate two full-sized automobiles; a carriage with two horses was more like it. But, as with most of the other small obstacles she and Matt had encountered after moving into their new apartment, Lisbeth and King had been more than cooperative in helping them overcome them.

Lisbeth had been a godsend to both Matt and Chris, but especially Chris, who had arrived in San Francisco uncertain of her job plans and not knowing a soul. Matt, her husband of eight years, already knew many of his colleagues in the San Francisco branch office because he'd gone there numerous times for meetings before the firm had offered him a permanent position on the coast. Even under the best of circumstances Chris felt that a man's transition to a new home was always easier than a woman's—it was the wife who usually had to find the new dry cleaners and food markets, the new doctors and dentist, and hire a housekeeper. To accomplish all those chores she considered herself lucky to have had Lisbeth's recommendations. She had not only become their landlord, but a friend as well.

The apartment was just right for them, it was spacious, full of Victorian charm, and it was located in Pacific Heights, the most prestigious residential section of the city. The front windows faced out on a park that occupied a full square city block, and from the tall windows in their bedroom they were treated to a view of Lisbeth's pride and joy, her garden. "All that beauty without any of the maintenance," visitors to the apartment would say each time they came. "How lucky you are." Indeed they had been very lucky to find such a place.

After settling into their new living quarters, Chris had had no trouble finding a better position in banking than the one she had left in Chicago. Matt had also done even better than they had hoped. Within six months of their moving to San Francisco, he had been put in charge of the entire West Coast operation. He traveled now more than she would have liked, but the trips weren't long, and he seemed to love the challenge of his new job.

On the surface, their life together seemed pretty good. Chris was in her late thirties, Matt was in his early forties. They were both physically attractive, made substantial salaries, took regular ski and sun vacations, read all the current books, and were up-to-date on Hollywood's latest efforts. They played a fierce game of mixed doubles, and occasionally threw gourmet dinner parties that had their guests talking for weeks afterward.

They fit everyone's ideal of a perfect couple. But they were a couple, not a family. Chris would gladly have made any sacrifice asked of her if she could change that. Matt had somehow resigned himself to their situation. After all they had been through—her two miscarriages, the in vitro treatments, which had never taken, and their one disastrous foray into the complex and, for them, heartrendingly disappointing arena of adoption—Matt had simply stopped discussing the subject.

Chris knew all too well that the unsuccessful adoption attempt, when the birth mother had changed her mind at the last minute, had nearly cost them their marriage. Thankfully, the disastrous adoption attempt had come just before Matt's transfer, which made it easier to leave the house and the fully furnished nursery they had prepared for the baby. If Matt ever found out that she had secretly packed the diapers and layette sets, the baby blankets and newborn necessities, he would be furious.

He would be even more furious if he discovered that a few weeks after they'd arrived in San Francisco, Chris had telephoned the Department of Social Services, and made an appointment to meet with one of their advisors.

She'd sat in a dingy office, facing a stern-looking woman. "And I want to learn all I can about the adoption laws here. I'm pretty familiar with the way it works in Illinois, but I'm totally in the dark here."

"I don't know anything about Illinois," she replied. "Did you adopt there?"

Chris hesitated for a moment, but then decided not to get into her past with this woman.

"No, we didn't. We ran out of time because my husband

8 6   T r a c y   S t e r n

was transferred here," she lied. "But I had started the process by advertising for a birth mother who might want us to have her baby."

The woman frowned. "Well, there's a fundamental difference right there. In California it is against the law to advertise for a baby. Absolutely, positively forbidden."

"Oh, my, that is a big difference. How does one go about finding a birth mother then?"

"Agencies, or a great stroke of luck. And sometimes this department gets listings, but not very often, and not for the kind of baby you want."

Chris was on her lunch hour, and was dressed nicely. The Social Services counselor had obviously sized her up as someone who would only accept a newborn, preferably of the same race as she was.

Suppressing her irritation, Chris continued. "If one is lucky enough to find a baby, how long does it take before the adoption is finalized?"

"It all depends," the woman replied. "Usually six months or so, but some have been known to drag on for more than a year."

Chris was astounded, and not at all encouraged by this news. "Really, you mean the birth mother can change her mind at any point during that time?"

"Less than one percent of adoptions are ever contested, Mrs. Brooks, let alone reversed," stated the counselor confidently. "Fifty percent of parents change their mind before giving birth. Another fifteen to twenty change just after giving birth."

"Yes, I know, but if you're part of that one percent it can be a very tough experience. In Illinois—" she began, but was interrupted.

"Mrs. Brooks, you're no longer in Illinois. In some states once the birth parents give their approval, assuming the father can be found, that's it. No turning back. But not here. When the birth mother signs the release papers in the hospital it only means that she has given over physical custody of the child. Then the process actually begins. But once she has signed the release papers she cannot withdraw that consent except with court approval. So, you see, as an adoptive parent you do have some protection."

"I see," Chris responded, but without much enthusiasm.

She left the office feeling emptier than ever. How horrible, she thought, knowing firsthand how tough it had been to lose the child they had been counting on even before they had seen her. Imagine the heartbreak that would be caused by having to give up a child you had thought was yours forever.

In any case, no matter what she had discovered, even if she found out that there were a million babies available, Matt would not even take part in a conversation on the subject, let alone consider attempting the process again. For him, the subject was closed, for now and forever. He had vowed never again to suffer the hurt of being so deeply disappointed.

But Chris was unable to ignore her desires, and each month when her period arrived precisely twenty-nine days after the last one, she would sit alone, mourning the loss of yet another chance to fulfill the constant longing that never completely left her. The hurt of being without a child was with her during every waking hour. It was a dull, constant pain similar to an aching tooth, which eventually would have to be attended to, but for a while was tolerable. The pain was never completely erased, and at times, when she passed a children's store and her eye caught the adorable little garments in the window, when they went skiing and saw the proud mothers and fathers guiding their own down the bunny slopes, even when she looked out her kitchen window to the park and saw the mothers and nannies attending to their children, she felt a pang so forceful she sometimes had to turn her eyes away.

Now as she stood in her kitchen unpacking the groceries, she looked across the street and was surprised to see Lisbeth sitting on one of the park benches. Lisbeth rarely sat in the park, but there she was, basking in the warmth of the late spring day. Next to her was a beautiful young girl whom Chris had noticed last week as she was entering the house. She wondered who she was, maybe a young research assistant from the magazine. Whoever she was, she certainly was pretty. The sunlight caught her long golden hair and created a halo effect around her head. The girl was smiling and talking, but all at once her expression turned serious and a look of sadness came over her. She turned to face Lisbeth, and Chris sensed that the nature of their conversation had changed dramatically. She was fascinated by the two women, and wondered about their connection to each other. The ringing telephone cut short her speculation and dragged her away from her observation post at the window.

• • •

"Kerry, it's been over a month, nearly five weeks now," Lisbeth began. "As hard as it is, it's time for you to make some decisions. The baby will be here before you know it, and you've got to start making plans." They had organized the medical end of things. Lisbeth had called her friends, and, in turn, they had called their own daughters and granddaughters, and soon a list of doctors had been compiled. Kerry had selected Dr. Rosen, an old-timer, who claimed he'd delivered half of the population of Pacific Heights, and then some. She felt comfortable with him and followed his advice to the letter. Soon she would start her Lamaze classes, which Lisbeth had agreed to attend with her. Also, she would soon know whether the baby was a boy or a girl, although from the very beginning she'd been certain it was a boy.

Kerry looked at her grandmother, knowing full well that she was right. Still she wasn't able to face the situation head-on.

"It's wonderful having you here, and you've been so helpful to me, to all of us," Lisbeth added. And indeed she had been. Kerry had begun to research Lisbeth's column, which made Lisbeth's life ever so much easier and her columns chock-full of great information. Lisbeth was pleased that her editor had noticed the improvement in her column, and she gave Kerry the credit that was due. It boded well if Kerry really wanted to pursue a career in journalism.

Kerry was never in the way. Mostly she stayed in her

own room, except when she went out for long walks, which sometimes lasted for hours. Lisbeth hoped that during these solitary times she was slowly coming to terms with her situation. Still, Kerry hadn't come to her with any concrete plan about what was going to happen when the baby arrived.

"Kerry, I believe you know that your options are limited. I truly wish I thought you were in a position to keep the baby, to raise it on your own, but circumstances being what they are, I don't really think that's feasible. If you had already completed your education, or had a job where you could afford help, or even a good day-care program, that would be another story. But it just isn't the case."

Kerry turned to her grandmother. Her expression told Lisbeth she wasn't hearing anything she didn't already know. "I know, Grandmother, but still, I can't believe you're suggesting that I give up my baby," she began. "To whom? To a pair of total strangers? This baby is the only part of Brad that I have left. Every time I think about it, I just can't bear the thought of giving the baby away . . . I just can't bear it," she said, tears streaming down her face.

"I know how hard it is to think of it, dear, but you must also think of the child. It truly wouldn't be fair to struggle to raise him or her, all on your own. That's not to say that you won't be meeting someone who will love the child as you do, but you can't count on that right now. Kerry, you have no idea how difficult it will be, even if you have the support of your family. Speaking of which, I think it's time we called your mother and asked her to come here. I feel as if I'm holding you hostage, and that it is unfair to her that she doesn't know about any of this. She is, after all, your mother." Lisbeth saw the anger begin to flare in Kerry's eyes, but she couldn't wait any longer to discuss these pressing issues.

"Kerry, soon you're really going to start to show, and then you won't be able to go back home without the whole world knowing. Now, I've promised you that you can stay with us until the baby is born, and I intend to keep that promise, but after that it is only fair that you make a plan for yourself. I've decided that in two weeks time I am going to call your mother and ask her to come here for a visit. Of course, you can make the call yourself if you prefer. Think about it and let me know how you feel. Whatever you're most comfortable with is what we'll do, but I feel we have to let her know what is going on."

"I'm not ready to call Mom just yet. Please let's wait a little longer," she pleaded. "I'm afraid she won't be much help in making any sort of decision. I'd rather settle that before she comes. I'll work it out, I know I can—I just need a little more time."

With that, Kerry got up from the bench and walked off into the park.

C h a p t e r   1 2

In the next two weeks, Lisbeth gave Kerry all the breathing room she felt she needed to make such a momentous decision in her life. Lisbeth was convinced that the right choice for Kerry was to give the baby up for adoption. She didn't want Kerry to compromise the rest of her life by being tied down with a baby at such a young age. She wouldn't be able to complete her education, or have a career. How many men would be attracted to her if she was saddled with a young child? Years ago, Lisbeth had learned to live with Nancy's modest ambitions, with her seeming inability to make her own decisions, but now she dared to hope for much more for her beloved granddaughter.

If Kerry insisted on raising the baby on her own, Lisbeth was prepared to support her decision. Whatever happened, she wanted her granddaughter to make up her mind herself. She would never be able to live with herself if she felt she had forced the young girl to make a choice that she might regret for the rest of her life.

Ever since their conversation in the park, Kerry spent less time around the house. By the time Lisbeth went down to breakfast in the morning, she had already left for the library, most often to do research for Lisbeth's column. She wouldn't return home until dinner.

"I certainly hope she's doing more soul searching than researching," Lisbeth said to Mary one morning.

"I hope so too," Mary agreed. "Maybe you'll find out more today. Her appointment with Dr. Rosen is at eleven. I reminded her before she left. She said she'd be back by ten."

Kerry and Lisbeth had made a habit of going downtown together for her doctor's appointments. King would drop Kerry off at the doctor's office, and take Lisbeth on her round of errands, until it was time for her to meet Kerry for lunch. Lisbeth looked forward to these outings; they always tried a new restaurant and Kerry also seemed to enjoy the break from their normal routine.

A little before ten Kerry returned and went upstairs to change her clothes. When she came down Lisbeth was shocked to see how pregnant her granddaughter looked. They hadn't seen much of each other during the last two weeks, but in that time the baby had really begun to show. Now, unless she wore very baggy clothing, anyone who saw her wouldn't have the slightest doubt that she was indeed with child.

Kerry smiled at her grandmother's reaction, and folded her hands across her protruding belly.

"I know," she said, smiling. "I've really grown. 'Popped' I think is the correct terminology. It seems that during the last few days this little fellow is really beginning to take shape. He's certainly active, that's for sure. Been kicking up a storm in there, keeping me up most of the night."

"All the signs of a healthy baby," Mary commented, patting Kerry on the back as the two women left the house.

•   •   •

Lisbeth sat with her second iced tea and checked her watch yet again. Now she was beginning to worry. She knew how busy Dr. Rosen's office was, but usually Kerry was no more than ten or fifteen minutes late in arriving at the restaurant. Now nearly a half hour had passed since the time of their reservation, and Lisbeth's imagination kicked in. What if they had found something wrong with the baby? What if the doctor needed to do something immediately, and Kerry had to go through the procedure all alone? She scolded herself for not having gone with Kerry.

After another fifteen minutes, Lisbeth was beside herself. Just as she was getting up to call Dr. Rosen's office, Kerry came rushing into the restaurant. One look at her and Lisbeth knew that all her fears were unfounded. Kerry looked radiant.

"I'm so sorry, Grandmother. I just couldn't help it. I know I should have called," she said, hanging her backpack on the chair and sitting down.

"Relax, dear. I must admit, during the last five minutes panic started to set in, but when I saw you come in, all my fears were put to rest. You look wonderful. I hope the doctor's report was good as well."

"I'm fine, Grandmother. Fit as a horse, Dr. Rosen says. But I have to watch my weight. I've gained five pounds since my last visit, so that puts an end to my late-night snacking. But the baby's still right on schedule, due the last week of September. The exam was mostly routine, but then I asked for some extra time to discuss something with Dr. Rosen. I'll tell you about all that later, but first I want to apologize for my behavior the last two weeks. I know that I have been impossible, probably unbearable, and I want to thank you for being so patient with me. I think if I had been treated the way I have treated you, I would have told the person in no uncertain terms to get out of my house. But as always, you've stuck by me; you've done more than I have a right to expect. I just needed some time to be alone and to make some decisions. So please forgive me, I'll try not to be such a burden ever again."

Lisbeth reached across the narrow table and took Kerry's hands in hers. "It hasn't been easy for any of us, dear. Mary and King have been as worried about you as I have, but I urged them to stay out of your way, and let you have the breathing room I felt you needed to make such a hard decision." Lisbeth stopped at that, hoping now to hear what Kerry had decided.

"So you will forgive me then?"

"Of course, Kerry, we all will. But tell me, what did you discuss with Dr. Rosen?"

"Well, I've decided that you're right. I'm in no position to take on the responsibility of a child at this point in my life. No matter how much I would love to keep Brad's baby, I could never give him the life I would want him to have. The life he deserves. Not right now anyway. So I've decided to find a couple who will take the baby. Take him and love him, and provide him with all the things I want him to have."

"Oh, dear," Lisbeth said, tears coming to her eyes. "I am so proud of you. Giving the baby up for adoption is the right thing to do, not only for the baby, but for you as well. This way you'll be at peace knowing that the baby is in a good home, and you can then carry on with your life. First you must finish school. Then find a career, not just a job. Gretchen has been so pleased with your work that I think that when the time comes, if you decide to stay in San Francisco, she will be willing to help you. You have so much ahead of you, so much to look forward to."

"That's how I feel too. So I spoke with Dr. Rosen about it," Kerry said, removing a large folder from her backpack. She cleared away the glasses and bread plate to make room for all the papers. "I'm afraid I've cheated you a little this week. Instead of finding new and exciting gardening information, I've been researching how the adoption process works in California. I wanted to find out as much as I could before I started. It's really not that complicated. Getting past the emotional issues is the hardest part. I asked Dr. Rosen if he knew of anyone who was looking for a baby, but he suggested going through one of the agencies. The most important thing is that the baby go to a couple who can give him the kind of life I'm just not capable of giving him right now.

"You used a phrase earlier that I don't agree with, though. You said 'giving the baby up' for adoption—what I want is not to give the baby up, as if I'm throwing him away, but I want to give him to someone. I want his new mother and father to have faces and names. I want to know where they went to school, and what they do for a living. I want to be a part of their lives. I couldn't just turn my baby over to a set of faceless people and then never know what happened to him. Does any of this make sense to you?" she asked, reading Lisbeth's quizzical expression.

"In a way. I must say, it's certainly different from the way adoption used to work. In the past everything was a big dark secret. The mother never knew the identity of the adoptive parents. Only in rare cases was it disclosed. The baby was born, turned over to the new parents, and that was that. The case was closed. If in the future the child wanted to find out more about his or her real parents, it was very difficult; it took a very compelling reason, and a court order, to open the sealed records. I guess everyone felt at that time that it was the best way to handle a difficult situation.

"You'll have to forgive me, dear, for being so old-fashioned. This is going to be quite a learning experience for me, for all of us, I think."

"If anyone can change and adapt, it's you, Grand-mother," Kerry said with a knowing smile. "You're the most up-to-the-minute grandmother a person could hope for. Don't worry, I'm learning along the way too. Last week I visited two adoption agencies. One I didn't like at all. The women who worked there were all in a hurry and only seemed to be interested in signing me up to give them my baby. It reminded me of those high-pressure sales pitches they give you at health clubs. But the other agency is terrific, and I'll go with them. I met with two of their counselors. Both of them seemed to care about me, as well as the baby. We talked for a long time; they asked me loads of questions about my family and about Brad. They reviewed with me a document they refer to as the birth parent's bill of rights. It's a list of fifteen different things that a birth parent has a right to expect from the process—things about medical care, the right to choose the parents, the right to talk with other women who have placed their babies in adoptive homes, the availability of counseling services even after the baby is born, and the most important aspect to me is that I will have the right to request pictures and updates about how the baby is doing. I can also pass along pictures and letters that I want him to have. The agency will forward any medical records that could be important to the child in the future."

"That's all helpful," Lisbeth agreed, "and it must make you feel very secure in your dealing with them. But how do you go about finding a family?"

"Elaine, the counselor who's been assigned to me, gave me all this information on some of the couples who are currently trying to adopt," she answered, pulling out file after file from the big envelope. "It's sort of a dossier on the people, what they do, how they live, if they have other children. They're also allowed to write anything else that they think might be of interest to a birth mother. This one got a little carried away," she said, pulling out a thick, bound folder. "The woman wrote about fifty pages describing her thoughts on motherhood. I'll probably stay away from that one—she might never let the baby talk."

Lisbeth laughed with her. They looked at their menus and gave their orders to the waitress before Kerry continued.

"All adoptions in California are open, to various degrees. Some even have the birth mother live with the adoptive family for a while after the baby is born, but I think that's going a little too far. I just want to select a couple, get to know as much about them as I can in the short time I have left, and then be able to leave the baby with a clear conscience."

Lisbeth was astounded by the amount of information Kerry had amassed during her visits to the library. She produced article after article about adoption.

Lisbeth listened intently to her every word, but as she did her concern grew, not about what she was hearing, but about the way Kerry was saying it. She sounded too removed. Too uninvolved. The way she spoke didn't reflect the emotional distress Lisbeth knew she must be feeling. It sounded as if she was talking about a school project, and was carried away by the facts she had learned. Not for one minute was Lisbeth convinced that Kerry realized how difficult it was actually going to be to give up the child after it was born. After all, as she had said herself so many times, this baby was all she had left of Brad.

As they left the restaurant Lisbeth hooked her arm through Kerry's and they walked out into the bright sunshine.

"I asked King to pick us up at Union Square," Lisbeth said. "I thought a little walk would do us good on such a sparkling day."

"I agree," Kerry said.

The streets were filled with shoppers and the flower stands were packed with colorful spring bouquets. They stopped at their favorite one and Kerry picked out two bunches of daisies.

"I'll take these home to Mary as a peace offering. She's worked so hard to make all my favorite foods and I haven't even been eating them. I've really been a monster," she said, tucking the wrapped bundle into her backpack, and climbing into the car after her grandmother.

As they started to pull into the driveway Lisbeth leaned forward to speak with King.

"Oh dear, after all that's gone on today, I forgot to pick up the things Mary asked for. Would you please drive over to the little store on the corner and I'll just dash in for a minute."

"I'll go with you," Kerry offered helpfully.

The little store was a lifesaver for those who lived in the neighborhood. Its aisles were stocked from floor to ceiling with a huge assortment of groceries. They charged a premium, but it was easier than going all the way back down to the big grocery store. Kerry and Lisbeth walked up and down the aisles filling Mary's order. Lisbeth was searching for a specific type of cereal when she heard a familiar voice.

"This place is a godsend, isn't it?"

"Indeed, it is," she answered before turning around.

"Oh, Chris, it's you," she said, finally abandoning her search. "I knew I knew the voice, but just couldn't place it."

Kerry stood behind her grandmother, holding the shopping basket.

"How good to see you. I've missed you during the past few weeks. I suppose we've all been busy with one thing or another."

"I know I have," Chris agreed. "Work has been a nightmare lately." Her eyes traveled to Kerry.

"Oh, Chris, I don't think you've had the chance to meet Kerry, my granddaughter. She's here visiting for a while. Kerry, meet Chris Brooks, she's our upstairs neighbor."

"Kerry," Chris said warmly, extending her hand and looking at her enviously. "I'm so happy to meet you. I must admit my curiosity has been working overtime. I've seen the two of you sitting in the park from time to time. Now I understand perfectly. You must have been planning for the arrival of your baby. It's wonderful! What an exciting time in your life. Congratulations. When is he or she due?"

Suddenly, Kerry withdrew her outstretched hand, as the tears filled her eyes. The two women watched as the cheerful expression on her face turned to one of pain and torment. She practically dropped the shopping basket, and then ran down the aisle and out of the store.

Lisbeth watched in shock as her granddaughter disappeared.

"Oh, I'm so sorry," Chris said, looking deeply concerned. "I didn't mean to upset her."

"You didn't say anything wrong, dear. Unfortunately, Kerry's pregnancy isn't the happy event it should be. You see, she was engaged to a nice young man, and then she became pregnant, by mistake. But the most horrible thing happened. He was killed in an automobile accident before she even had a chance to tell him. Maybe you even remember reading about that terrible accident in Tahoe. So she's come to stay with me until the baby is born." Lisbeth sighed, tiredly. "Just today, she told me that she's decided to put the baby up for adoption. She's already seen a counselor at one of the agencies, and she's carrying around résumés of prospective couples. So you've caught her at a very tough moment."

"I still feel so badly for having upset her," Chris replied. "I can imagine what pain she must be going through. It's so difficult for a young girl to make such a tough decision. I just didn't know."

"Of course not, dear. You couldn't have. Don't worry. Kerry is going to have to get used to the idea of the adoption. I only hope I can help her through it. I thought that today at lunch she was acting far too calm and controlled, and now I see that she was on the verge of exploding. Your harmless comments were just too much for her."

"Please tell her how sorry I am," Chris said. "I hope we'll be able to see each other under happier circumstances. I'm familiar with the whole adoption process. Matt and I tried to adopt a baby right before we moved from Chicago. Unfortunately, it wasn't a very pleasant experience for us. I'm sure Kerry's will be different. She's so lucky to have you to help her through it."

Lisbeth smiled back at the young woman who had become such a good friend to her. "Please don't give this another thought. I'm sure that in a few days Kerry will have adjusted to her decision and her emotions will be at a lower pitch. Maybe then we can all get together for tea."

"I'd like that," Chris said, before Lisbeth said good-bye and headed for the checkout counter.

Chris remained with her own basket and watched as Lisbeth went out the door and into the waiting car. She finished her own shopping in a daze, and in spite of Lisbeth's advice not to give the encounter another thought, by the time she arrived home her mind was racing with visions of Kerry and her baby.

Chapter 13

Kerry sat on the bed in her room, staring out the window but only seeing a vision of Brad's handsome, smiling face. She had cried until she had no more tears, and now she felt an overwhelming sense of sadness. She feared that by making the decision to find a couple to adopt her baby she was letting Brad down in the worst possible way.

Rationally, she knew her decision was the right one, but emotionally she was having trouble dealing with it. The terrible scene with her grandmother and her neighbor had proven that all too dramatically and painfully. She just hadn't been able to bear answering questions from a stranger, especially one who so obviously viewed her pregnancy as a joyous event. Kerry knew that Chris had only been trying to be nice and that she didn't know the whole story, but nonetheless, she had found her enthusiasm so horribly inappropriate and upsetting.

Still, Kerry knew that she had to begin to face the enormity of her decision, and she started by reviewing all the applications that Elaine had given her.

"These are couples who we feel might be appropriate for your baby," the counselor had told her during their second meeting. "We've gone through all of our listings of couples who are waiting for babies, and I hope some of these people will appeal to you. These profiles will give you an idea of the lifestyle, religion, and education that would be offered to your child. If any of these couples interest you, we can schedule a meeting with them. You know that you don't have to make this decision before the baby is born, but from our last conversation, I got the impression that you are committed to finding adoptive parents as soon as possible. Don't hesitate to call me anytime, about even the smallest thing."

Elaine put her arm around her shoulder and walked her to the door of the agency. "Kerry, we all know what a monumental decision this is for you. Remember, you must feel comfortable with all phases of the process. Think back to that birth parent's bill of rights we went over. It's your baby. We're here to help, and to support you all along the way, and afterward as well. We want a partnership with you. If you decide to go through with this, as I told you earlier, we're going to meet often, maybe as many as six or eight times over the next three months. After the baby is born those meetings will continue. We want you to be able to go on with your life, to live with this decision forever. It's going to take time, lots of time. You will experience a period of loss and grief, and that's only healthy. If you didn't we'd all be very concerned about you. But we're here for you—we're not going to abandon you at any point during or after this process."

Kerry liked the women she met at the agency. They were all intelligent and caring, and realistic in their attitudes about life. Most of them were mothers themselves, so they knew what they were talking about when they spoke about the delivery, and the overwhelming sense of loss they warned her she would feel as she left the hospital alone, without the precious newborn she had carried for the better part of a year.

"We're very concerned about the fact that your fiancé was killed," Elaine had said. "You were very much in love with him, and his death alone is an enormous loss. Now you're talking about experiencing another loss, practically right on top of that one, and we know how traumatic that can be for a young woman. You must really think this thing through and let us help you along the way. But only you can make the final choice."

Elaine's words echoed in Kerry's head as she reviewed

the résumés she had given her. Several she eliminated right away. She didn't want a couple who already had a child. She wanted her baby to be the center of attention for a loving couple. She selected two applications that sounded good to her—both were young couples in their mid-thirties who had tried to have children of their own, but for whatever reason had been unsuccessful. Her heart went out to them as she read the descriptions of the painful, devastating, and often very expensive process of dealing with their infertility. One woman described her feeling of emptiness and failure at her inability to conceive in such dramatic terms that Kerry's eyes began to tear. But she knew that sympathy was not the right reason to select a couple, so she moved on to the next application. She especially liked the note that one of the women had attached to the papers, describing the nursery room in which the baby would live, and all the things the couple would look forward to doing with the child as he or she grew up. The woman had written about festive birthday parties and Christmas holidays, which she promised would be filled with love and laughter—and prettily wrapped presents. Kerry drew a big star on the first page of this one, and hoped that the woman was as good a person as she was a writer.

She had just begun to make a list of questions for the two couples she had selected when she heard a light knock on the door. Lisbeth stuck her head in cautiously.

"Oh, Grandmother, come in. I was just finishing up here and was going to come downstairs in a minute."

"No rush, darling, I just wanted to check on you, to see how you are feeling."

"I'm all right. I'm sorry for this afternoon."

"Don't worry, dear. Chris did call to check on you, and she's very sorry that she upset you. But I told her not even to think about it. How could she have known? She's such a dear girl, and she was really beside herself with worry for you. She hopes that when you are ready we can all get together for tea. She and her husband are very familiar with adoption; they tried it once themselves. I don't know what happened, but something must have gone wrong, since they don't have any children. Perhaps when she comes down for a chat we'll ask her."

"That would be nice. I'd like to meet her again under better circumstances. I feel so badly about having run out like that, but I just couldn't help it. Hearing her enthusiasm was too much for me to handle."

"That's a completely honest reaction, which is easy to understand. Time is the only thing that is going to ease that feeling. Now let's get on with it, shall we? Are you hungry at all? Mary has dinner waiting for you."

"Yes, come to think of it, I am. I'll be right down. I just want to finish writing down my thoughts about this couple. Maybe you can help me, if you would. Out of all the applications, this couple sounds the friendliest, and most like the parents I might select for my baby. He likes sports and describes himself as an 'urban jock,' sounds a little like Brad. He might be good especially since I'm almost certain that it's a boy. I'll know for sure next week. She sounds very sweet. Read how she describes the birthday parties and holidays she would plan for her child."

Kerry handed the papers to Lisbeth. Delighted to be included in the process, Lisbeth took a seat in the small slipper chair by the dresser.

"We'd love to welcome a newborn into our home," the letter began. "We would treasure him or her, and nurture and love the baby as if it were our own. For so long we've had a void in our lives. We've tried everything possible to have a child of our own, but the realization that we will never have one will not diminish the love we would have for an adopted child. We both attended college and have professional careers. A good education for the child would be a top priority for us."

Lisbeth finished reading and put the papers down in her lap. She looked over at Kerry, who remained cross-legged on the bed, continuing to write in her notebook.

"These people sound very nice, very interesting, and they certainly have the right ideas," Lisbeth began, "but one can't possibly tell from an application what they're really like or determine if they're truly good people. Will you be able to meet them, on their own turf, so to speak, before you decide?"

"Of course," Kerry answered, closing her book and putting it aside. "Once I decide that they are candidates, the counselor sets up a meeting, first at the agency, and then later at their home, if they agree. Anyone who didn't agree to a home meeting would be off my list pronto. I definitely want to see where the baby is going to live. They also have to agree to have what they call a 'home study.' This is done by a representative of the Department of Social Services. Someone visits their home, checks it out, asks tons and tons of questions, and basically pries into the most intimate details of their personal lives. Sometimes this can be very trying for the couple; they don't understand why they have to divulge so much information, but the state requires it. It's done to protect the child."

"Well, you've made a good start, in any case. When will you meet with Elaine again?"

"She said to call when I'm ready. What's nice is that they don't try to force you into making a decision too quickly. The only real deadline I'm up against is the baby's birth. If you're going to find someone to adopt, it's best to do it before the baby is born. Elaine has said that I can wait until afterwards, but I don't think that would be fair to anyone. Imagine taking the baby home, living with him, and then having to turn him over. I don't think so. So I want to move the process along. I think I'll call her and set up a meeting for later this week."

"Good idea," Lisbeth agreed. "But don't forget I've promised Gretchen that we'll drive up to her house in Napa for lunch next Saturday. I think you'll enjoy it and it's also a chance for you to talk to her about working for the magazine, if you have that in mind. Besides, it will do us both a world of good to get out of the city for a day."

Gretchen Wagner was the senior editor at *Gardens & Homes* magazine where Lisbeth's gardening column had originated. Kerry had developed a friendship with her over the phone when she had started helping Lisbeth with her research. Once Kerry had mentioned her interest in journalism, and Gretchen had offered to help her find work, maybe even at her magazine. Kerry had been thrilled. Under normal circumstances she would have looked forward to meeting Gretchen in person, but in her current state she dreaded it. Still, in order to avoid disappointing her grandmother, she vowed to make the best of it.

Chapter 14

By the time Chris heard Matt turn his key in the front lock, she had worked herself into a frenzy. Not even the harsh knowledge that Matt had no interest in trying adoption again could temper her excitement. She was convinced that they were the perfect couple for Kerry's baby. She had always believed in the fates, in serendipity, and all the signs led her to hope that she and Matt would become the baby's adoptive parents. After all, hadn't she and Kerry met for the first time on the very day Kerry had decided to find a couple to adopt her child? The only problem Chris could see was that she was hoping alone, and that was not enough to make the adoption a reality.

Chris was sitting in the living room, and as she heard Matt come down the hallway she lowered the paper she had been holding for nearly an hour, but had barely glanced at. He kissed her on the cheek. She looked up at him, gave him a warm smile, and tried in that split second to assess his mood. Matt was not the most handsome man she had ever known, but he was certainly the one who had charmed her, and after their very first date she'd reported to her best friend that Matt was the man she was destined to marry. The courtship hadn't always been smooth, but finally she had gotten her man. She had never regretted her choice, even in the darkest days of the adoption saga.

"How was your day, little lady?" he asked, as he loosened his tie and walked toward the kitchen.

She held back the urge to scream out that it had been fantastic, that she had met the young woman who would give them the child they longed for, and that the woman lived right downstairs, right under their very noses! She caught herself just in time, wanting him to relax for a minute, and have his nightly glass of wine in hand, before she even broached the forbidden subject with him.

"Fine, the usual, they are making me crazy with the reports. We did them over for the fifth, and hopefully last time today. I did leave a little early in frustration."

"Ah, the arduous life of a banker," he teased, returning from the kitchen with his glass of wine, plus one for her.

"Thank you, sweet," she said, accepting the glass. "And your day?"

"More of the same. Jack's acting up and may have to be shipped back to Chicago. Let him suffer through a few more winters and mellow out before he is allowed to return to paradise," he said, speaking only half-seriously about this partner and friend who had transferred with him from the Midwest. He settled into the chair opposite her and disappeared behind the sports section of the newspaper.

Matt finished his wine and the newspaper at the same time. As he came toward her to take her glass for a refill, she decided that the moment was right to tell him about the real event of the day.

"I ran into Lisbeth today," she began, cautiously.

"How is she?"

"Fine, busy as always. She was with her granddaughter, Kerry. A beautiful girl. They were coming back from lunch together, and had stopped at the corner store where I was picking up a few things."

"Yes, I've noticed that girl coming and going. I wondered who she was. She's pretty."

"Yes, she is young and pretty, and very pregnant. It's such a sad story. Her fiancé was killed in a car accident up in Tahoe before she even had a chance to tell him that they were going to have a baby. She was too afraid to share the news with her parents, so Lisbeth agreed that she could come and stay with her until the baby was born. It's a shame that it happened, and an even bigger shame that her relationship with her parents is so poor that she couldn't turn to them."

"It is too bad," Matt agreed, "but it's not going to be any

easier to hide the baby after it's born. What's she planning on doing then?"

Chris was immediately disappointed, but as she had feared, Matt's thoughts were not moving in the same directions as hers.

"She's planning to give the baby up for adoption." There, she had uttered the venomous word. "Only today did she finally tell Lisbeth that she had made her decision. She's already seen a counselor at the top agency here, and she's starting to review applications from prospective parents . . ." Her voice trailed off, but she knew Matt had detected her excitement.

"Chris, you aren't starting up with this idea again, are you?" He was staring hard at her now, challenging her to deny the thoughts she had been thinking all afternoon.

"Yes, Matt, I am. In fact, I think it's the perfect situation. The last time was a terrible stroke of bad luck. But this time it's practically fallen into our laps. It seems to me that it couldn't be more right for us. We know the girl is Lisbeth's granddaughter, so she must come from a nice family. I'm sure she had a good upbringing. She didn't go out and get pregnant during a one-night stand. She was engaged to marry the baby's father. If he hadn't been killed, there's no way on earth this baby would be available for adoption. Don't you see, Matt, if we don't follow up on this, and right now, a baby who could be just right for us could end up going to another couple. Won't you please consider this?"

She watched as the rage grew in his eyes.

"Chris, I can't believe you'd even mention this to me. First of all, you don't even know the girl. You met her for five minutes in the aisle of a grocery store. So she's giving up the baby for adoption. So what?" he yelled. "It happens every day, and just like what happened to us, young girls change their minds, disappointing couples who have been gullible enough to believe that adoption is a way to get a baby they can't have, and probably shouldn't have. No. Absolutely not. I thought we closed the book on this subject long ago. Don't you recall how horrible it was, or have you completely blocked that from your memory? I really don't want to hear another word about it."

His words enraged her. She would not take no for an answer, not about something that was so vital to her life.

"You're not being fair," she shot back. "It's not as if I've gone out and tried to find us another child. I didn't approach anyone; this is just a stroke of wonderful good luck. That's how I see it anyway. Do you know how long it's been since I've stopped at the corner market to shop? It's been ages. Don't you think it's odd that today I met Lisbeth and Kerry, and that she had only today decided to offer her child for adoption? I believe that things happen for a reason, and the reason in this case is that we could adopt her baby."

"You're full of nonsense! The reason you stopped in the store is because you forgot something at the big market. The fact that Lisbeth and this girl were there means absolutely nothing. If your life is guided by mere coincidences, we're in more trouble than I thought."

"You're being totally and completely unfair," Chris countered. "I don't think you realize how important this is to me. I know we had an unfortunate experience, but that's not a valid reason for giving up on adopting a child."

"Unfortunate?" he shouted, raising his voice several decibels. She was certain that if Lisbeth and Kerry were at home they could hear every angry word being said. "Do you really call what we went through merely unfortunate? It was like having our guts ripped out. It was the worst experience of my life. Have you forgotten all those sleepless nights, all the days when you had to wear sunglasses to work, claiming you had an eye infection? Your eyes were so swollen from crying that I thought you'd never recover. Have you forgotten the day the call came that wiped out everything we had counted on? All the planning, the anticipation, the shopping for all those clothes that no child would ever wear? All the meetings and discussions, all the totally ridiculous efforts to explain why we wanted what most people are usually able to have without consulting anyone else? And what about the horrible woman who came to do the home study? She asked questions even my mother would be too embarrassed to ask. And that's saying a lot. I will never ever subject myself to that kind of scrutiny again. This time it would be even worse. They'll say we're too old, and that you work too many hours, and I travel too much to be a good parent. They may not even like the color of our new sofas," he added sarcastically. "It's none of their business. Just because we can't produce a child doesn't mean I have to put myself under a stranger's microscope. No,

Chris, I won't even consider it, and that's the end of it. The end, do you understand?" He sank into his chair looking exhausted.

"No, I don't understand, Matt. What if the adoption had worked out as the majority of them do? Wouldn't the whole long, upsetting process have been worth it then? Wouldn't we have forgotten all the bad parts? It would have changed our life forever."

"It did change our life forever, only in a negative way."

"This time could be so different, I just know it. We'd be getting permission directly from the mother, not from some intermediary. We have a chance this time to work directly with the birth mother—we can ask her beforehand if she is absolutely certain."

"Chris, I said no, and I mean no. I gave up on this idea long ago."

"Then you've given up on us," she shot back.

Matt got up out of the chair and headed down the hallway to their bedroom. When he returned minutes later, he was dressed for a run.

"I'm going out," he said, coldly.

"I've made dinner. How long will you be gone?"

"Until you've gotten this ridiculous idea out of your head. Once and for all," he answered, walking away.

Chris jumped as the front door slammed behind him.

Chapter 15

The sound of rain beating against the windows awakened Kerry on Saturday morning. She lay in bed hoping that the storm was sufficiently strong to cancel their trip to the Napa Valley. But her hopes were quickly dashed when she heard Lisbeth talking to King, making plans for the day.

"With this weather, we'd do well to leave a few minutes early," Lisbeth suggested. "Then again, you never know, once we cross the bridge it could be sunny and warm."

No such luck, Kerry groaned to herself, then turned over and pulled the covers up under her chin. I'll have to go and face these people. At least the cool weather would provide her with an excuse to wear a big sweater that would conceal her tummy.

Lisbeth's predictions came true, and just as they crossed the Golden Gate Bridge into Marin County the clouds disappeared and the sun came out.

"Beautiful," Lisbeth commented as they neared Gretchen's home. "I hope she'll be serving lunch outdoors. It's such a spectacular setting. And don't be shy about asking her about the magazine, and what role you might be able to play there. Several times she's asked me what your plans are come September. Maybe if you decide to stay here you could go to school and work part-time for her. Wouldn't that be nice?"

"Do you know who else will be there?" Kerry asked as her nervousness mounted. She hoped it would be just the three of them, but she'd heard Lisbeth inquire about Gretchen's husband and family.

"I didn't ask, but I'm sure Gretchen's husband will be there; I've only met him once or twice, but he's very charming; and maybe one of the children. I haven't seen her son in years; he's been off at college and hasn't been home much. Of course she may have invited some other friends as well. I'm certain it will be a lovely afternoon. She entertains with great style, and as you can tell from your conversations with her, she's really very nice."

Gretchen came out of the house with open arms. "Welcome, welcome," she said, embracing Lisbeth and giving her a big hug. "And Kerry," she said, "my budding journalist, how great to see you. This telephone stuff can only go so far."

"How nice to meet you also," Kerry responded, self-consciously pulling at her sweater and fidgeting as Gretchen looked at her. Now that she was meeting Gretchen in person she dreaded that the woman would notice that she was pregnant and start questioning her. *When is the baby due? Who's the father? I didn't know you were married.* But nothing remotely like that happened as Gretchen led them inside into a large living room, which was both spacious and pleasantly decorated. Kerry loved being in other people's homes. She loved looking at the things they had chosen to make a place their own. This room was very much a reflection of Gretchen's love of family. Silver framed pictures dotted nearly every available surface, and the handsome furniture looked comfortable and inviting. She felt at home here. This was the type of home she hoped to find for her baby.

Kerry started to relax until she looked out the French doors, which gave way onto a large deck. There she saw that the table for lunch was set for many people. Six, seven . . . She stopped counting when Gretchen asked her what she would like to drink. Startled, she looked up at her.

"We're all having champagne and orange juice, if that inspires you," Gretchen offered.

"Just some water, thank you."

"That we have in great quantity."

Drinks in hand, the three of them toured Gretchen's gardens. While Lisbeth examined them with a professional's eye, commenting on Gretchen's talent, Kerry tried to stop worrying about who was going to join them for lunch. The suspense ended shortly, first with the arrival of two black Labs who came running out of the bushes, right in the direction of Gretchen's lily garden.

"The calm and serenity of the day is over," Gretchen announced, moving quickly to reroute the Labs before they flattened out the plants. "Betsy, Igor, over here," she called. "I've warned you two." She sighed. "I hope you like dogs," she said to Kerry as the Labs broke away from her and raced toward Kerry.

"More than anything," Kerry said as she knelt down to greet the two mischievous canines. Their bodies shook all over in excitement, and they nestled into her arms, nearly knocking her over. Rubbing their heads and gratefully accepting their wet kisses, Kerry smiled, feeling happier than she had in ages.

At the sound of new voices, she looked up to see a tall, very elegant man, with curly dark hair that had just begun to gray at the temples. His blue workshirt was open a few buttons, and his well-worn jeans were covered with chaps.

He offered his hand to help Kerry up from her position on the terrace with the two dogs in her lap. Immediately she was self-conscious again, and she tugged at the sweater around her waist before accepting his outstretched hand. He pulled her to her feet with one strong motion.

"We usually don't allow our animals to throw our guests to the ground. I hope you don't mind," he offered. "By the way, I'm Jack Wagner, Gretchen's husband."

"Nice to meet you," Kerry answered. "And no, I didn't mind at all. In fact, I encouraged it. I have a dog at home, it's just that he's not quite as active as these two," she said. "They're wonderful animals." Suddenly she longed to see her own dog, Senator.

"Well, we think so. They're especially keyed up right now because they've been out with the horses. My son is visiting with two of his friends, and as soon as the weather cleared we went riding. The dogs keep up with us, and then they come back in the afternoon and collapse. What you're seeing is thankfully the last of their energy for the day. Soon they'll be under a tree, dead to the world."

At the news of Gretchen's son and his friends, Kerry started to feel nervous again.

"Here they are now," Jack said as a younger, taller version of himself approached. "Josh, this is Kerry. She's survived the attack of the beasts. They had her on the ground."

Josh held out his hand to her. He had the same dark good looks as his father, and she decided on the spot that in twenty years he would be much more attractive than he was right now. "Nice to have you here. If you'd come earlier you could have joined us on the ride. It was great. You do ride, don't you?" he said suddenly, as if he might have assumed something that wasn't true at all.

Kerry smiled at him, liking his spirit. "Yes, I do ride," she answered, again all too aware of the sweater she was wearing. I must look like an idiot, dressed like this in this warm weather, she thought. "It's been a while, but if you're raised in Nevada, you usually do spend time on a horse. I miss it," she admitted.

"Well, we'll have to make a plan for the next time you come up. Mom said you might be working at the magazine in the fall, and I'm here a lot, now that I'll be back in school in San Francisco."

Their conversation was interrupted when Josh's friends Allison and Donny joined them and Gretchen called them all to the table for lunch.

"Beautiful enough to photograph," Jack said as he took his place at the head of the table. "You could use this in next month's magazine. I enjoy lunch even more knowing it can be written off," he joked, and everyone laughed.

The table did look beautiful, Kerry thought, as she examined the place settings and masses of summer flowers arranged carefully in big ceramic vases. Plates of chicken breasts, grilled vegetables, and an enormous bowl of salad were passed around. Being with a family made her long for home once more. She tried to put those feelings aside and enjoy herself. Everything was going just fine until the baby began to kick. Kerry was convinced that everyone's eyes were immediately drawn to her stomach, but after a few minutes, as the conversation continued, she began to relax.

She was surprised by the way Josh and his friends monopolized the conversation. In early September they would begin their first year of law school at the University of San Francisco. They all seemed to be very impressed with themselves as they traded quips and wittily held forth about their goals, their sure-to-be-overloaded class schedules, and the number of students who wouldn't make it past the first year. Of course, there seemed to be no doubt in any of their own minds that they would ace their first year, Kerry observed. They were at the top of their game, certain that they would succeed. Their self-confidence stood in stark contrast to her own confused feelings. She hadn't a clue about what she would do in the future.

By the end of the meal Kerry's first opinion of Josh had changed entirely, and she was anxious to leave. Because Josh and his friends had dominated the conversation, she and Gretchen hadn't had a chance to talk about journalism and she didn't want to leave without at least expressing some interest in working at the magazine. Finally, when Josh and company left the table, Kerry had an opening.

"The lunch was wonderful, Gretchen, but I'm sorry that we didn't have a chance to talk more about the magazine. You've been so wonderful to me, and I want you to know how much I appreciate it."

"Yes, it did go so quickly. All this chatter about law school. They are so excited and apprehensive about it right now, and sometimes it's hard to curb their enthusiasm—shut them up is what I really mean," she added.

Kerry smiled. "Yes, but it's terrific to be so excited about school. I'm really looking forward to getting a job that I can be as excited about. Of course, I'm going to have to go to school at the same time."

"Not a problem," Gretchen answered. "I can find work for you on a part-time basis. You just let me know when you're ready to start. I'll line some things up for you in no time."

"I can't tell you how much I will appreciate that, how much it will help me," Kerry answered, and the look Gretchen gave her in return told her that somehow the kind woman understood how much her help would mean to her.

Their good-byes said, Lisbeth and Kerry settled back into the car for the ride home.

Kerry's thoughts once again turned to Brad, and how much she missed him. Josh was about his age, maybe a year younger, but what a different personality and temperament. Brad was gentle, courteous, and soft-spoken. He would never have enjoyed dominating a conversation and talking on and on about himself the way Josh had.

"See, it wasn't so bad," Lisbeth said. "You made it through the day and no one said a word about your pregnancy. No one even noticed."

"Thanks to the camouflage," Kerry answered, patting her sweater. "There were some rough moments, though. The baby was really starting to kick fiercely at lunch. Must have been the peppers in the salad.

"But you're right, I didn't have to answer any questions, didn't even have much of a chance to talk."

"You noticed that too?" Lisbeth asked. "I thought maybe it was just me. I haven't spent much time around young people lately. Did you think they talked a bit too much about themselves?"

"A bit? How about way too much. At first I thought that Josh was a nice guy, but I sure changed my mind about that. He's way too impressed with himself. It's as if law school is the biggest thing that could happen to a person. And his friends all acted the same way. But Gretchen and her husband are delightful. I was lucky to have half a second to talk to her about the magazine."

"Yes, I was so glad you finally got a chance to speak with her."

"The day did make me realize one thing, though . . ." Kerry felt her eyes fill with tears.

"What darling?"

"It made me think about how much I miss everyone, Mom, Dad, Willy, and especially Amy. I even miss smelly old Senator," she sighed, unhappily. "Meeting Josh and Donny only brought back memories of Brad," she added. "I've been living such a lie for the past five months, and it's starting to take its toll. I think it's time we invited Mom to come over. I have to face the truth sooner or later, and I think now is the time to start."

Lisbeth reached over and patted her hand. "I'm very proud of you, dear, that's such a big step forward. I'll be happy to call your mother if you want me to, if it will make it any easier for you. I know that once she sees you, and everything is out in the open, it's going to be a lot easier on you. You'll see."

"I hope so. Within the next six weeks or so, I have to decide about the adoptive parents, and have all the papers ready, just in case the baby comes early. Once he's born, everything has to be in order."

"It will all fall into place," Lisbeth assured her.

Kerry nodded her agreement, clutching her stomach as the baby began to kick furiously once again.

PART
IV

Chapter 16

"If you feel good about Marjorie and Allan, maybe you should go ahead and choose them," Elaine said in that comforting, caring voice that was beginning to annoy Kerry. It was already August and she couldn't understand why Elaine hadn't yet found a couple she really liked. So far, after interviewing six couples, Kerry hadn't felt that any of them were perfect for her child. Four she had eliminated practically on sight; the fifth had been doing all right until they'd told Kerry that her baby was only the first of many they planned to adopt. They wanted five, maybe six children, and Kerry was so put off by the idea that her child would be part of a tribe of unrelated infants that she cut short the interview and fled their house as quickly as she could. When she'd asked the prospective father in the sixth couple what kind of activities and sports he would teach his child, he'd responded brusquely, "There's a playground down the street." Kerry had immediately drawn a thick black line through their application.

The worst part of the interviews was that even though the people made an effort to be pleasant, Kerry still left each meeting feeling that she had been reduced to a commodity, another birth mother who was going to produce a product that each couple was desperate to have. Despite what they said, Kerry didn't think that any of them had a clue about what she was going through. So far, she hadn't connected on any level with any of the couples she'd interviewed. She couldn't imagine turning her baby over to any of them.

Walking to the bus stop after two disappointing interviews and the frustrating meeting with Elaine, Kerry was overcome with anger. She hated Brad for dying. She hated him for making a turn in front of the big truck. How could he have been so stupid; he knew those roads well enough not to have made such a dumb, tragic mistake. It was so unfair of him to leave her like this, alone and with no one to help her deal with this crisis. She longed for him to be by her side as she walked along, so she could hit him and scream at him, and then fall exhausted into his arms. If only, if only . . .

As quickly as it had come, her anger passed and was replaced by an overwhelming sense of guilt. She hated herself for thinking those terrible thoughts about Brad. As she waited for the bus, she ran through a litany of regrets that pierced her heart. Why had she been so adamant about where they sat at the movies that it had escalated into a fight? What difference did it make if he forgot to pick up something she had specifically asked for? How could she have expressed disappointment about the kind of flowers he had lovingly selected for her to wear to the senior prom? Why had she made such a fuss over trivial matters? She hated herself for all the petty arguments she started and the mean things she'd said. She wished more than anything for a chance to make it all up to him. The worst memory was how abrupt she had been during their last phone call. The last time they would ever speak. If she had it to do all over again, she would be so much nicer, she would overlook so many small things that she had made issues of. Most of all she would want them to make love more often, for those intimate moments were the ones she treasured most. She climbed onto the bus still thinking about how she would do things differently. If only, if only . . .

The kitchen was empty, but the remnants of preparations for tea were still out on the counter, so Kerry headed toward the library in search of Lisbeth.

She assumed that Lisbeth had company, but it never occurred to her that it might be Chris. Her first reaction, upon seeing them deep in conversation, with tea cups balanced on their laps, was to turn and head straight up the stairs to the privacy of her room. But she remembered how rude she had been to Chris in the market, and Lisbeth, seated in the big winged-back chair near the fireplace, had already spotted her.

Lisbeth was in her gardening clothes, khakis and an old sweater. Kerry had never seen her entertain in this outfit, so she assumed that Chris had paid her grandmother a surprise visit.

"Why, Kerry, you're . . . here . . ." Lisbeth said, sounding flustered and most unlike herself.

"Yes, I am," Kerry answered, entering the room. "You sound so surprised! I am a bit early, but I said I'd be back about now."

"Yes, I suppose you did, dear. Well, in any case, welcome home. Chris and I are just having a cup of tea. Get yourself a cup and join us."

Before returning to the kitchen for another cup and saucer, Kerry said hello to Chris, who also seemed a bit flustered at her sudden appearance.

Maybe it was just her imagination, but she felt as she came back into the room that the two women had been whispering to each other while she was gone.

"Kerry, Chris wanted to come up and talk with you today, but she asked to speak with me first," Lisbeth began.

"Yes, I did, but I may have made a wrong decision. I suppose that maybe I should have come to you first. I feel that now I've put your grandmother in a very awkward position."

Lisbeth made an effort to smooth the way. "Not at all, Chris. After all, you only met Kerry for a brief moment, and not under the very best circumstances. It is you and I who have gotten to know each other over the past year. No, I'm not in an uncomfortable place. I just want the best for everyone, as you can imagine. In any event, now that she's here, why don't you tell Kerry why you've come."

Chris sat up straighter in the chair, obviously preparing to say something that was both important and sensitive. She leaned forward and placed her cup on the coffee table, and then folded her hands in her lap. "First, I want to apologize for upsetting you in the market. I just didn't know."

"Of course not, how could you?" Kerry offered quickly, trying to make this as easy as possible for Chris. There was so much she liked about her, the way she looked, the gentle way she spoke. Kerry also knew what a good friend she had been to Lisbeth, and how caring she had been during the rough times with Charles. "Don't say anything more, it's all forgotten. During the last few weeks I've learned to be much stronger about all of this, and my time is running out," she continued, patting her round tummy, "so I no longer have the luxury of getting so upset about things. I'm just searching for a couple who will be the best parents for my baby."

"That's why I've come, Kerry. I would like you to consider Matt and me as potential adoptive parents for your baby."

Rendered speechless by this sudden and completely unexpected idea, Kerry could only stare at Chris.

After what seemed like ages, Lisbeth tried once again to smooth the road. "That's what Chris and I were talking about when you came in," she offered, "and Chris was very concerned that you would be upset that she came to me first to ask about it, but I assured her that you would not be upset at all. After all, this is a bit, well, let's face it, it's very unexpected, and I don't have any idea how you feel about it."

Kerry remained silent, trying to gather her thoughts.

"Well, Kerry?"

Finally, she said, "I'm just as surprised as you must have been, Grandmother. Of course it never occurred to me that Chris and Matt were considering adopting a child. This is all so new to me, and I am so involved in working with the agency that . . ."

"Of course, I understand," Chris spoke again. "And I will certainly understand if you want us to work through the agency. That is, if you would consider us, and also if you haven't already made up your mind about someone else." She waited, breathlessly, for Kerry to answer.

"No, not at all, I haven't found any couple who I'm crazy about."

Chris looked relieved.

"I think I would like to speak to Elaine about this. She's the woman at the agency who has been helping me," she added for Chris's benefit. "But why don't you tell me a little more about your plans, and why you'd like to have my baby?" Kerry suggested.

For the next hour, Chris told Kerry everything that she had been thinking since their chance meeting in the grocery store. She spoke about her love of children, about growing up in a large family with lots of activity and pets and never a dull moment in between. She spoke candidly about the problems she and Matt had experienced, the heartbreak of her miscarriages and the devastating experience with adoption.

Kerry listened patiently, and her sympathy grew when she saw the unshed tears in Chris's eyes as she spoke about the phone call they'd received from the birth mother, telling them that she had changed her mind about the adoption.

"Suddenly it was all off, everything we had planned on. I was just thankful that we hadn't seen the baby yet. I think if we had, the pain would have been unbearable."

"I'm so sorry that it happened to you," Kerry said. "It

must have been awful, but I've heard that from time to time a mother finds it impossible to give up the baby. I guess there are as many different reasons as there are mothers, but in my case, I just know that adoption is the right thing to do. It wouldn't be fair to anyone if I changed my mind, least of all to the baby."

"I'm happy to hear you say that," Chris answered, and then added somewhat anxiously, "Kerry, can you tell me what you think about my idea? I don't want to push you, but I would like to know if we at least have a chance. We'd really make very good parents."

"I'm sure you would," Kerry agreed politely. "It's just that this is all very unexpected. Were you actively trying to adopt again when we ran into each other in the store?"

Chris hesitated, and Kerry saw her stiffen in the chair. She had struck an emotional spot. "Well, no, not exactly. You see, the one and only time we tried to adopt, it ended so horribly that we had really given up on the idea. That is, Matt had given up, but I never did. I always wanted to try again."

"What does Matt think of this idea?" Lisbeth interjected.

Once again Chris hesitated, and then sat back in her chair, looking deflated. "I must admit, he's not crazy about it. In fact, he's adamantly opposed to it."

"Oh," was all Lisbeth could manage.

"That's a serious problem, Chris," Kerry said. "I don't know if we can even talk about your adopting the baby if Matt isn't completely on board. Also, I've never even met him. If he's so opposed to this, I don't suppose he would be very interested in talking to me. I haven't found the perfect couple for my baby, but at least I have been meeting couples who are in agreement that they do want a child. I just don't know . . ."

"Believe me, it's my biggest worry also. But I know that if I try hard enough, I can make Matt see my point and agree with me. In the beginning he wanted a child as badly as I still do. In fact, he's the one who pushed to do the adoption. He took it much harder than I did when the girl changed her mind. Now he's dead set against it. The only reason I am so adamant about trying again is because this time I thought I could get to know you, the birth mother. Because you are the granddaughter of a friend of ours. This time I know it will be different. Now I just have to convince Matt that it will be, and then he'll want this as much as I do. Oh, Kerry, I'd bet my marriage on this, I know I can make him feel the way I do. I will need your help though."

"How so?"

"Of course you'll have to meet Matt. I know you'll love him, he's warm and generous, and would make a wonderful father. You will just have to convince him that you're not going to change your mind on us, that once you decide that we will be good parents for your baby, you will live with the decision you have made. You two will have to spend some time together. Once he hears it from you, rather than from an intermediary like before, then I'm sure everything will be just fine."

Beyond Chris's enthusiasm, Kerry still detected a note of concern and trepidation in her voice. "Oh, Chris, I don't know. It seems to me that if you haven't been able to work it out between the two of you, my coming and talking to him wouldn't make much difference."

"It will make all the difference in the world, I promise. Will you at least think about it?"

Kerry looked at Chris and saw the sincerity in her eyes. She longed for a child, it was clear, and nothing would make her happier, short of having a child with Matt, than having Kerry's baby. Of that she felt certain. But Matt was another issue, and whether or not he could be convinced remained to be seen.

"Yes, I will, Chris. I can't say that I'm not concerned about Matt, but if you say he can be convinced, I will certainly give it a try. Now, please excuse me, it's been quite a day, and the baby is starting to kick again. I think I need to lie down for a little while."

"Of course. I'm sorry, I should have been more aware of how you were feeling after running around all day. I know this must be difficult for you, all of this. Coming here like this is completely out of character for me. If I hadn't felt so strongly about it, I never would have ventured down here."

Lisbeth stood up to walk Chris to the door.

"Get some rest, Kerry," Chris added before she left. "And please call me when you're ready to talk. I look forward to it."

Kerry remained in the big chair long after she heard the

door shut. Moments later, Lisbeth returned with a fresh pot of tea.

"Well, what do you think?" she asked her grandmother.

"Oh my, these things are never as simple as they seem, are they?"

"Never," Kerry agreed, shifting her weight around and trying to find a position that was comfortable. "But I do like Chris very much, and she's been such a good friend to you."

"That's no reason to give her your baby," Lisbeth shot back. "You must only consider it if it feels right, and if you think they would make good parents. Otherwise you should continue your search through the agency."

"Well right now we're only dealing with one parent. That's a problem."

"It certainly is. I don't know Matt as well as I know Chris, but she must know if he can be convinced or not. It sure seems that she is committed to the idea."

"Adoption takes two completely committed people," Kerry responded, "otherwise it will never work. Plus they would never make it through the home study and the interviews at the agency. If the counselors detect one iota of hesitation on the part of either person, that couple is out the door and off the list. There are just too many people trying to adopt these days."

"Dear, it is a difficult decision under the best of circumstances, but I think it's worth a try. My biggest concern is not that they would make good parents, but that they live upstairs from me. It means that you would have to get your own apartment before you have the baby. It would be too difficult for you to come here from the hospital. It's just too close for comfort. Of course, that's not a problem, you were planning to find a place of your own anyway, but we'd just have to see to it a bit earlier than planned, is all. Don't you agree?"

Kerry saw it all in her mind, her baby being brought here, but instead of coming into Lisbeth's home, he would be taken upstairs by his new parents. It was more than she could bear. "Yes, you're right. There is no way I could be here, knowing that the baby was so close. No, that would never do. Never." She sighed. "I think I would like to go up and lie down now. It's all been very tiring today, two interviews, the meeting with Elaine, and now Chris." Kerry lifted herself slowly out of the chair, feeling as if she was carrying triplets. Her legs were swollen and her back ached from sitting in one position for so long. "I feel like an elephant. A pregnant elephant." She sighed again.

"I know, dear, but soon it will be over, and you'll have your lovely figure back," Lisbeth said encouragingly.

"You're the greatest," Kerry said, leaning over to kiss her grandmother's cheek.

"You'll change your opinion shortly," she said. "I've one more item to add to your agenda."

This stopped Kerry cold in her tracks, and she turned from her position on the third stair to look back at Lisbeth.

"Your mother arrives tomorrow night."

Chapter 17

The three women sat in the library, the room that Lisbeth always chose for serious discussions. Its small size and the way the chairs were arranged around the fireplace forced everyone to sit very close to each other, and to confront the issues at hand.

Lisbeth was in her normal spot by the hearth, and Kerry and her mother sat side by side on the loveseat. A tense silence had fallen over the room. After the initial shock of seeing Kerry in her full-blown state, her mother made a few nervous comments. It was obvious that she didn't know what to say, or couldn't say what she was really thinking. Now Nancy McKinney sat eerily still, her hands folded in her lap.

Kerry looked from her grandmother to her mother, feeling more amazed than ever at the enormous differences between them. Lisbeth was a take-charge individual, and one always felt that no matter what challenge she was presented with, she would rise to the occasion and face it.

Kerry could tell from the expression on Lisbeth's face that she was allowing Nancy to digest the shock of seeing Kerry just a month away from delivering a baby she knew nothing about. She had already helped Kerry immensely by telling her that adoption was the route she had decided to take. As soon as her grandmother determined that enough time had passed for Nancy to absorb the news, she would, as she had done many times in the past, rub her hands together, sit forward in her chair, and insist that the three of them look on the bright side of things, make the necessary plans, and simply move on.

Her mother, on the other hand, Kerry thought, seemed to be waiting for someone else to take the lead, to make the decisions and basically tell her what to do. She had always been that way. It was the main reason why Coach had become such a domineering force in their family life. Even if her mother disagreed with him, in the end she always went along. Kerry could not remember a time when her mother had stood up for what she wanted, held her ground, and made her own wishes come true.

Kerry felt that for a long time there had been an emotional distance between herself and her mother. Kerry loved her mother a great deal and knew that her mother had always been loving and kind to her. She just wished that Nancy had more backbone and inner strength.

Slowly Nancy turned to her daughter. "Why didn't you tell me?"

The pained look on her mother's face tore at Kerry's heart. Kerry hesitated until she felt certain her voice wouldn't fail her. Anticipating this exact confrontation, she had rehearsed these words so many times. "Oh, Mom, I just didn't feel I could. Dad was so devastated by Brad's death, I didn't want to upset him even more. You know how conservative he is. He'd feel so ashamed that his daughter was going to have a baby out of wedlock. I knew you would understand, that it was a terrible mistake, and that we never meant for this to happen. But I couldn't ask you to keep this secret from him. It would have been too much to expect."

Nancy sighed before she spoke. "Kerry, your father and I love you very much. You are our daughter. We would have found a solution."

Kerry leaned over and put her arm around her mother. So unused to hearing her declare her feelings about anything, she was touched by what she had said. "Of course you would have, Mom. I just felt that it would be so much easier and better for everyone if I left for a while, to have the baby away from Carson City, and Brad's family, and all the memories. Maybe it was selfish of me." Kerry paused for a moment and then continued. "Anyway, I was lucky enough that Lisbeth said I could come and stay with her. She's been wonderful, she's helped me every step of the way, and besides, she's kept me plenty busy. She put me to work on the column about the second day I was here."

Nancy managed a sad smile. "Still, I wish . . ."

Kerry interrupted. "Mom, there are many things I wish too. I wish that all of this had never happened, that Brad hadn't died, that I wasn't facing a whole slew of decisions that have to be made very quickly, but I can't dwell on any of those wishes now. Now, I have a little more than a month to tie up a lot of loose ends and figure out what I want to do with the rest of my life."

Lisbeth felt like applauding. The girl was holding her

own, showing a strength of character that Lisbeth admired. It would have been so easy for her simply to have collapsed into her mother's arms. Instead, Kerry had faced down, in a mature and loving way, one of the biggest obstacles she had been avoiding. Now Nancy knew that Kerry was going to have a baby and that she had decided to give the baby up for adoption. Kerry had put a major hurdle behind her and could move on to the next.

"Well, I for one have worked up an enormous appetite after all this," Lisbeth announced. "Mary has made a wonderful lunch, and it's nice enough to eat in the garden. Shall we?"

They sat outside in the midst of Lisbeth's pride and joy, in the brilliant sunshine, and Mary served them lunch. Lisbeth and Kerry ate heartily, but Nancy sat quietly, staring at Kerry's enormous tummy.

"Mom, please stop staring and eat. It's delicious," Kerry said, helping herself to more salad.

Nancy looked up at her, obviously confused and hurt by her daughter's comment. "I can't help it if all this has come as a great shock to me. After all, you two have had a chance to get used to the idea. For quite some time, I might add." She shot a glance in her mother's direction.

"Nancy, let's not start in about that. It has been hard on all of us, I can assure you, and now it is time to work together and make the best of a difficult situation." That said, Lisbeth returned to her meal.

Kerry, determined to see the glass half-full, spoke about her plans. "I'm really leaning toward Chris for the adoption.

I thought about it a lot last night, and of all the possibilities, she is the best."

"What about Matt?" Lisbeth asked, concerned.

"I'm going to talk to him tomorrow. Chris says they've had several more discussions, and although he's not fully on board yet, she still is convinced that it's going to be okay. After all the people I've met, and all the conversations I've had, I don't think any couple is going to be perfect. I feel safer going with Chris, even though Matt might not want it as badly as she does."

"If that's the case, dear, then we had better start looking for an apartment for you very soon. I am adamant about your not coming back here from the hospital if the baby is right upstairs. Mary will make meals for you, and maybe your mother will want to come back then, so you won't be alone. I'll certainly be around, but as you know, I can't really leave Charles for any length of time."

Nancy followed their conversation back and forth, turning her head as if watching a tennis match. Kerry stopped for a moment and tried to recap her meetings with all of the couples.

"Adoption certainly has changed since my day," Nancy said, looking confused. "Before, the mother never even knew where the baby was going, let alone the name of the people taking the baby. Now it is all out in the open. I've never heard of the adoptive parents being in the delivery room with the mother. Unbelievable," she ended, shaking her head in a combination of disapproval and dismay.

"Mom, I fully expect that Chris will be in the delivery room with me. I want her to be there," Kerry said. "Just because it's not her own baby doesn't mean she shouldn't share in the birth of a child that will become hers. One of the couples I interviewed even asked if they could cut the umbilical cord. But that might be a little too much."

Nancy grimaced.

Kerry chose to ignore it. "I'm hoping that Chris will go with me to the last of my Lamaze classes. She said she wanted to, plus it would give Lisbeth a little rest. She's been such a trouper. You've been at every session, haven't you?"

"Haven't missed a one, and I'll be more than happy to turn that job over to her," Lisbeth replied. "Sitting on mats on the floor is too much for an old lady like me."

"This all sounds so complicated," Nancy blurted out. "If Chris and Matt aren't one of the couples from the agency, how will everything be . . . arranged?"

"The process remains the same, because I've already told Chris that they'll have to register with the agency. I've worked it out with Elaine, and as soon as I give the go-ahead, she will set up a meeting with them to organize everything. They'll still have to go through a home study, which I've heard is the worst part of the whole deal. Some stranger, representing the Department of Social Services, comes to your home to determine if you'll be fit parents. The questions they ask can be very personal and probing. Chris said that Matt really was upset that they have to go through all that again. But they do. And they will have to hire an attorney. There's a ton of paperwork to be filled out. After I sign what they call the statement of understanding papers, then the baby is released to them from the hospital. After that, it takes about six months for the adoption to be finalized."

"That long?" Nancy asked, incredulously.

"At least," Kerry answered. "Some have been known to take two years. Once it gets into the system you just have to wait and wait. It's like anything else—it's all the red tape of the bureaucracy. You wouldn't believe all the forms I have to fill out."

"Whose child is it until the adoption is finalized?"

"The baby will belong to Chris and Matt from the moment I sign the release papers, which is usually done in the hospital right after they take me back to my room. I still have legal responsibility until the adoption is granted in court, but once I sign those papers, that's really it. If I want to withdraw my consent after that, I would have to get approval from the court.

"I have a choice of staying on the maternity floor, or going to another wing of the hospital. It's up to me, and right now I don't know how I feel about that. Some mothers even decide to nurse the baby for a day or two. They say it makes it easier to say good-bye, but I think it would be just the opposite, and I don't want to do it. The doctor said they could give me a shot to make my milk dry up after I give birth. But the room situation is still one I have to let them know about."

Thinking about this question, which she had wrestled with over and over again in her mind, upset Kerry more than she had thought. She returned to her food, stabbing a piece of lettuce with her fork, but changing her mind as she lifted it toward her mouth.

Ignoring her daughter's sudden silence, Nancy continued with her inquiry. "Did you ever consider any other options besides giving the baby away?"

Kerry chose not to correct her mother's reference to adoption, which made it sound as if she were throwing the child out the window. "Yes, for a long time I hoped that I could figure out a way to keep the baby," she answered. "But the more I thought about it, and the more Lisbeth and I discussed it, the more I realized that it just wasn't possible. It wouldn't be fair, not to me or to the baby. I would have to give up my education, get a job, and try to support both of us on a meager salary. What kind of life would I be able to offer him? Plus, if I find a couple to adopt him, he can have a father. It was a tough decision, but I know it is the right one," she said with finality.

"You had other choices," Nancy responded.

At first Kerry thought that her mother meant she should go home and raise the baby there. But the cold look in her mother's eyes told her otherwise. Suddenly her mother's meaning hit her. "You mean, Mom, did I ever consider having an abortion and just getting rid of Brad's baby?" She couldn't disguise the tremendous hurt her mother's words had inflicted. What would possess her even to suggest such a thing? It wasn't that Kerry was opposed to abortion. She believed that in some cases it was the right thing to do.

But not now. This was not an unwanted pregnancy, just an unexpected one. She saw a world of difference between the two.

Trying to calm herself, Kerry waited a moment and then continued. "No, I really never thought seriously about it. It would have been like killing a part of myself. Don't you see that this baby is all I have left of Brad? I hope that someday, when the child is grown up, we might be friends, at least through letters if not in person, so I can tell him what a wonderful man his father was, how much I loved him, and how he died without even knowing that he was going to be a father." For the second time that day, she willed back the tears that flooded her eyes. But she was determined not to let her mother's reaction confuse her or shed any doubt on her decision.

"That's one of the reasons I'm considering Chris and Matt," Kerry said firmly. "Because I think I might be able to have a relationship with them that would make all those things possible.

"Would you like to meet them while you're here?" Kerry asked her mother, hopefully.

Not even turning her head to look directly at her daughter, she replied icily, "I think not."

Kerry was crushed. Her mother's unwillingness or inability to support her left her reeling. It also reinforced her belief in how right she had been to turn to Lisbeth in the first place.

Chapter 18

To say that it had been a total success would be an over-statement, but the first meeting between Matt and Kerry had gone better than Chris had expected.

"She's a very nice girl," Matt said in response to Chris's queries about the meeting. "She's everything you told me she was, and she seems serious about wanting us to have her baby."

Chris held her breath and waited for the objections to come, but they never did. "What does that mean?" she finally dared to ask.

"It means that I'm still not totally convinced about all this. Yes, she was able to look me straight in the eye and tell me that she was sure she wanted us to have her child, but I detected a lack of conviction in her voice. It was almost as if she was speaking for someone else, that she really didn't have anything to do with it. The only thing I feel totally sure about is that the father can't change his mind."

"Matt, that's ridiculous! And I'm going to ignore that comment about Brad. It's not funny."

His temper began to flare. "It may sound ridiculous, but I'm telling you how I felt. I think she's probably had so many sessions at the adoption agency that she's working on automatic pilot."

"I think you're being unfair."

She could hear him take a deep breath before he continued. "I'm being honest. The impression I got is that she's working with her head, not with her heart."

"What on earth do you mean by that?"

"What I mean is that once the baby is born, and she sees him and holds him, it's going to be a lot tougher than she thinks to let us have him. She could always turn to Lisbeth and ask her for help until she can handle him on her own."

"I really don't think that's an option. Lisbeth has already told her that she has to find her own apartment, that she can't come back here after she leaves the hospital. No, you're wrong about all of this."

"I hope so, but I just want you to know what I'm thinking."

"Okay, I know, and I've had the same concerns, but I think it will all work out. So where does all this leave us?"

"It means that if it's what you really want, then I'll support you."

"Oh, Matt, do you really mean it?"

"Of course I do. I'll always have my fears. But you've made it very clear how much this means to you, and I'll try my hardest to put those fears aside. For you," he said, taking her in his arms.

She clung to him, thanking him with the biggest hug she had ever given him.

But he pulled back, and she couldn't recall ever seeing him look so serious. "Chris, we really went to the mat on this one. I can't forget that you as much as threatened to leave me if I didn't go along, and this should prove to you how much you mean to me. I don't know what will happen if this all goes wrong. I can't promise you that I have the strength for another massive disappointment."

"Nothing will go wrong, I promise. We're going to have this baby."

"I certainly hope you're right," he said. It was the most sincere statement she had ever heard him make.

The day after her mother left, Kerry finalized her decision to let Chris and Matt adopt her baby. Then she immediately went out to look for an apartment. It was hard to explain to landlords why she only needed a studio when it was obvious that she was about to have a baby, so after a while she told everyone she was looking for an apartment for her sister. Finally, after exhaustive searching, she found a cute little studio down in the Marina district, and she signed the lease on the spot. Her apartment was so small that it only took Mary a day or two to clean and organize it. Once that was done a moving company was hired to deliver the furniture that Lisbeth had offered to give her.

Kerry loved her new neighborhood. She could walk to do her shopping, to see Lisbeth (although she knew she wouldn't be going up to Pacific Heights too often in the near future), and she could take the bus downtown when she started her new job in October. Once she had told Gretchen that she was ready to go to work, Gretchen had kept her promise and found a spot for her at the magazine. She would start as an assistant, floating around the office and doing whatever odd jobs needed to be done, and from there she could chart her own career path, with Gretchen as a willing mentor. Gretchen had even agreed to let her work on a flexible schedule once she started school in January. Kerry felt a bit guilty that she still hadn't mentioned the baby to Gretchen, but she really didn't think it was necessary. Someday, if the time was ever right, she would tell her.

After Kerry had made all the arrangements for her new life, the days started to drag. She tried not to dwell on the fact that at this point in their pregnancies most new mothers were enjoying festive baby showers given by their friends, last-minute shopping trips for their baby's layette, and most important, love and support from their husbands. Instead of feeling sorry for herself, she began a diary to record her thoughts and feelings during the last few days of pregnancy. She would sit at Lisbeth's computer, which was on the desk that faced out into the garden, and type away. *It's important for you to remember that I put you up for adoption not because I didn't care, but because I did. I cared so much that I was willing to live without you if it meant that you could have a better life with someone else than you could have with me. That's the main thing you should know. The other thing you should know is that you are moving around and causing me so much discomfort right now that I would give you away to the first bidder, if anyone would take you. It seems a bit unfair that the birth mother has to go through all the pain of la-*

bor, and the adoptive mother is spared. She just waits on the sidelines for the nurse to hand her the baby. I'm going to work on changing that. She smiled to herself, hoping that her child would find the humor in what she had written. Someday she hoped to make the diary a gift to her son, assuming that he was curious about his biological mother and what she had been thinking just days before he made his entrance into the world, and she released him to those she had chosen to love and raise him as their own. She had just finished correcting what she'd written that day when the telephone rang. Knowing that she was working, Mary efficiently picked up on the first ring.

Seconds later the light on the phone was flashing and Mary buzzed her on the intercom. "It's for you, dear," she said, "and don't forget Chris and Matt are coming to dinner tonight. They're coming early because Matt is flying later this evening to Chicago. You might want to get in a little nap before then."

"Thanks Mary, I think I can make it through the evening. He's not kicking up a storm today."

"Pick up on line one," she said.

"Hello," she said, expecting Gretchen or someone from Dr. Rosen's office.

"Kerry? Mom tells me you're joining the magazine next month. Congratulations, I think it's great."

For a few seconds she drew a total blank. But then she put it all together.

"Is this . . . ?"

"It's Josh. Sorry, I should have said so. Sounds like I caught you off guard."

You certainly weren't who I was expecting to hear from, she wanted to say. "Well, I just wasn't expecting a call from you, that's all."

She waited for him to launch into a detailed report about his classes and all of the other boring minutiae that had practically put her to sleep when he'd talked at his mother's house.

"I was just calling to tell you I'm glad that you've decided to work with Mom, and that she's really looking forward to it. I can't remember her being so excited about having someone new on board. You'll have fun, and learn a lot from her."

"Yes, I already have, and I'm looking forward to it as well," she answered. Right after I give birth to a baby, give it up for adoption, move into a new apartment, and try to adjust to a new life, she wanted to add. She longed to get off the phone, but she couldn't be rude to him, even though her instincts were prompting her in that direction. Why was he calling, anyway? Not just because she was going to be a lowly assistant at his mother's magazine.

"I've thought about calling you ever since we met, but I've really been busy settling into school. It's just as tough as we all expected."

"I'm sure it will calm down soon, and you'll start to enjoy it more," Kerry said politely as she rolled her eyes.

"Hope so, but in the meantime, I'm going up to Napa this weekend and wondered if you'd like to come up for a ride. I can make up for leaving you out the last time. And I know Betsy and Igor would love to see you."

Kerry had to keep herself from giggling at the thought of her enormous self on horseback. She rubbed her hands over her stomach, held back her laughter, and said she was sorry, that she had other plans.

He sounded genuinely disappointed. "Oh, I'm sorry you can't come. It will be a while before I'm going to be able to get up there again. Maybe we can have dinner in the city sometime."

"Yes, maybe once I start work," she suggested, safely putting him off for at least a month.

"All right," he agreed, sounding as if he was getting the message that she wasn't anxious to see him.

"Thanks for calling," she said in closing.

"Take care, Kerry, and call if you change your mind between now and Friday. I'm not leaving until Saturday morning."

"I will," she assured him, again suppressing a giggle at the thought of herself going horseback riding, tummy and all.

Chris and Matt came for dinner, and, as planned, Matt left for the airport before dessert was served.

"Take care, Kerry, I'll be back on Wednesday. Try to hold the tiger back until then," he said warmly to her, patting her on the shoulder as he left the table.

Chris smiled broadly at his comments, and walked him

to the door. He kissed her, grabbed the small carry-on bag he had brought down with him, and went out to the waiting car. As she returned to the table, her smile stayed with her.

"I think he's not only adjusted to the idea, but he's downright excited about it," she said, sitting back down.

"Seems like it," Lisbeth concurred. "You would really have had your hands full otherwise. A screaming newborn and a grumpy husband is a lethal combination."

Kerry smiled weakly. She had been quiet all evening, and now was anxious to go to her room. With great effort, she stood up and said her good nights. She hadn't skipped a dessert in weeks, and this sudden change of habit was met with concern from all. "No, nothing's wrong, I just can't sit still anymore," she insisted. "This little fellow is kicking up a storm again. I'd like to lie down and give him a full playing field. See you in the morning."

"Sweet dreams," Lisbeth offered.

But her dreams were not sweet at all, and when she finally switched on the bedside lamp it was only two hours after she'd turned in. The little fellow had no intention of sleeping or letting her sleep tonight. The bed felt wet. Instinctively, she knew that there wasn't much time to spare.

She quickly dried herself with a towel, threw on a big sweater and baggy pants, and went downstairs to the telephone.

"Wake up, coach, you're on," she said when she heard Chris's sleepy voice on the line.

"Now? Oh, Kerry, wonderful! I'll get dressed and be down in a flash. We'll take my car."

"Yes, I'd rather not wake Lisbeth if we don't have to. Who knows how long the labor will be. But my water broke, and the contractions are pretty strong, so I want to get to the hospital soon. I'll call Dr. Rosen, then I'll meet you in the garage."

"I'm on my way."

It was certainly convenient having your birth coach right in the same house, Kerry thought, as another powerful contraction racked her body. She scribbled a note for Lisbeth and Mary, and then walked slowly out to the car.

Twelve hours later she delivered an eight-pound, ten-ounce little boy. He came out screaming and kicking, and she could barely catch a glimpse of him as he was passed from doctor to nurse and then to another nurse who was waiting to clean him up and wrap him in a blanket.

"All ten fingers, ten toes, very robust-looking," Dr. Rosen declared with a warm smile.

Chris wiped the perspiration from Kerry's forehead for the hundredth time that morning, and then for the first time she left her side and went to look at the baby who would become her son.

"Here he is, Mrs. Brooks," the nurse said as she handed the tiny infant over to her. Her tears drenched the surgical mask she was wearing, and she regretted that Matt wasn't there to share the moment with her.

Chris walked back to Kerry, clutching the baby to her. She laid him down gently next to her, and Kerry reached over to stroke his precious face, touch his tiny fingers.

"Sweet, sweet boy," she cried, through her own tears.

"Yes, he is, and we're going to take very good care of him," Chris added, not really knowing what to say. It was a moment that she would remember forever, not for the words, but for the looks she exchanged with Kerry.

The baby began to cry, a loud, healthy wail. The nurse appeared and took the baby from her side.

Kerry wanted to lift her head, but it was impossible, the labor had taken every bit of energy she possessed, and then some. Suddenly several men in green hospital gowns moved her off the table, onto a gurney. Then the gurney was moving, taking her out of the room. Taking her away before she was ready. She wanted to hold her baby longer. It was so unfair. She tried to protest, but no one heard her over the cries of the newborn.

PART
V

Chapter 19

The big field was filled with tall yellow flowers that blew softly in the wind. There were masses of them, each stem nearly three feet high. Kerry and Brad had walked into the field together, but then he had left her. Now she spotted him running back toward her, through the brilliant yellow sea, pushing the stalks aside as he ran. She too was heading toward him, although it seemed she was still miles away. He was yelling at her, but she couldn't make out what he was saying. The wind and the rustling noise of the flowers made it impossible to hear. But as they came closer to each other, she was finally able to hear him. He was frantic.

"Kerry, what did you do with him?"

For a moment she didn't know what he was talking about.

"Tell me," he shouted. "Where is he? I can't find him anywhere, but he must be here. He's got to be here."

Then she knew. He wanted to know where the baby was. She had told him that he was gone, but he'd refused to believe it.

"Show me what you have done with him! He's my son. How could you have given him away?"

She had tried to explain to him what had happened, but he wouldn't listen, and grew more frantic, running from her and searching for a tiny newborn in the vast field that stretched all the way to the horizon. Now she had to reach him so she could explain every-

thing, but as she started forward, trying to push her way through the flowers, they closed around her like a big yellow cage. They were as strong as steel. She was trapped. She reached out to take Brad's hand, but he had disappeared.

She awakened in a panic, confused by the dream, unsure of her surroundings. But then she shifted in the bed, and suddenly it all came back to her. She let out a little cry of pain as she tried to raise herself up on her elbows.

The room was darkened, but she couldn't tell if it was only because the curtains on the far side of the room, on the other side of her roommate's bed, had been pulled shut, or if she had really slept until night. It had been almost one o'clock in the afternoon when they had wheeled her down from the delivery room, despite her protests to stay with her baby for a minute. Then the nurse had given her a shot. It must have been some sort of sedative if she had slept until now.

Kerry raised herself up on her elbows, pushed back the covers, and climbed out of bed. She sat on the edge of the bed, and glanced over at her sleeping roommate. Now she remembered, the woman had had visitors earlier in the evening, a grown son and daughter. She had sensed that they knew why she was there, in a room far away from the maternity ward, far away from the baby she had given birth to only hours earlier. They had looked at her with a combination of interest and pity, and when their eyes met, Kerry had turned her face from them.

Now that she was awake she had to see her son. She had made a mistake in choosing to be moved away from the maternity ward. How terribly wrong she had been to think that she could spend the night so far away from him.

The lights in the hallway had been dimmed, giving the corridor an eerie feeling. Kerry checked in both directions before walking toward the elevators. She knew what she was doing was forbidden, but she couldn't resist.

She approached the nursery's protective glass. cautiously, apprehensive that if anyone spotted her they would take her back to her room before she could see her son. The baby beds stood in rows; there were so many of them. It had been a busy night at the hospital.

Kerry's eyes traveled from newborn to newborn, searching. Will I always be able to recognize him? she wondered. Even if years pass without seeing him, will he always be familiar to me? As her eyes darted from baby to baby, each identically wrapped in a pristine white cloth, she panicked. Which one *was* he? There were so many, and they looked so much alike, yet surely she would know him.

Just when she had nearly convinced herself that something terrible had happened to him, that he was sick, that he had required special care, her eyes locked on a baby in the first row. It was him! He was asleep, but she would know her son anywhere. Then she looked at the crib, and at the card placed at the front so that visitors would be able to pick out the new addition to their family. She recognized the last name of his new parents. All at once the finality of her decision struck her. It was done. Now there could be no turning back.

Kerry suddenly felt weak, her legs collapsing beneath her. She grabbed on to the ledge at the bottom of the window, trying to break her fall. Nothing, neither the many sessions with the counselor nor the late-night talks with Lisbeth, had prepared her for the overwhelming experience of childbirth. The bond she felt with this tiny infant in the crib before her was so much stronger than she had anticipated, perhaps even as strong as what she still felt for his father.

How will I ever be able to give him up? she wondered. How will I find the strength to keep my promise? In just two days, they will take him away. How will I ever find the strength to say good-bye?

Her questions echoed in her confused mind as she felt the gentle touch of the nurse's hand on her elbow.

"Come, dear, you must go back to your room now," she said softly, guiding her slowly away from the nursery.

Kerry looked back at the crib once more before turning away, then shrugged off the nurse's hand. Oh, Brad, what have I done? she said to herself as she headed slowly back to her bed.

Chapter 20

"This will take care of you right away," the jolly nurse said as she prepared the syringe on the little plastic tray. "Now just turn over, honey, and show me your backside for a minute.

"You'll be back down to regular size in no time, honey," the nurse said as she completed her assignment. "No use carrying all that milk around if you're not going to use it."

Breakfast arrived, and an hour later it remained untouched. She didn't feel like eating, she only wanted to be in the nursery with her son. Maybe since everyone was so busy, dashing from room to room checking vitals and dispensing morning orders, she could go down undetected. But after what had happened last night, the nursery staff would surely be on the lookout for her.

The meeting was set for two o'clock. She and Elaine, the social worker assigned to the case, Chris and Matt and their attorney would congregate in the small private waiting room on the floor where Kerry was staying, and in an hour at the most, they told her, it would all be over. Kerry would be asked a series of questions, which she had already reviewed with Elaine, then she would be presented with two documents, a statement of understanding that would show that she knew what she was doing, and a release form that would allow Matt and Chris to leave the hospital with her baby. Everything was set so that the adoption would proceed smoothly.

But as she sat staring at her breakfast tray, she knew she couldn't bring herself to sign the papers. She tried to pinpoint the exact moment when she realized what a crucial mistake she had made. Was it when they had handed the baby over to Chris in the delivery room, and then only allowed her to see him for a few seconds before they wheeled her away? Or was it in the middle of the night, as she watched him sleeping peacefully alongside the other newborns? Or was it the echo of Brad's voice in the dream, which had been as real to her as anything that had actually happened in her life? Why hadn't anyone told her about the tight bond she would feel with her baby? Or about the overwhelming love she'd feel for him? The other birth mothers and the counselors she had spoken to had said it would be difficult, but no one had warned her that it would be heart-wrenching.

She picked up the phone to call Lisbeth; she would start with her, and go down the list from there—Elaine, Chris, and then Chris's attorney.

While she was waiting for an outside line, she heard the door to her room swing open.

"Did you have a good rest? You certainly deserved it." All of a sudden Chris was by her side, her arms holding an enormous bouquet of flowers. She wore a pair of gray flannel slacks and a yellow cashmere sweater. Around her shoulders she had tied another sweater, this one a dark blue. She looked like a woman who didn't have a worry in the world.

Kerry couldn't believe that Chris had brought her flowers and was acting as if there was something to celebrate. She deeply resented her insensitivity. Before she even spoke, it dawned on Chris that she had made a bad move.

"Maybe I shouldn't have brought flowers," she said, looking down at them. "How thoughtless of me." She put the big bouquet of lilacs, tulips, and roses on the chair next to the bed.

"I'm sorry, I really wasn't thinking, you probably don't feel like flowers right now. Were you able to get some sleep?"

"I can't do this," Kerry said, in a voice that was barely more than a whisper.

Chris heard her the first time, but didn't want to believe it. The birth mother she had come to count on had just uttered the words most feared by adoptive parents. She had changed her mind. "What did you say, Kerry? I didn't hear you."

Kerry hated her. Here she was, beautifully dressed, her hair freshly washed, her face perfectly made up and her only obligation for the day was to attend a meeting that would finalize her plans to go home tomorrow with the baby.

Kerry, on the other hand, was tired, her hair matted down from yesterday's perspiration, and she was wearing the standard hospital-issue gown that barely covered her still very heavy body. All she had to look forward to was going home, alone, to a tiny apartment. There she would sit and grieve for her lost son while just a few blocks away Chris and Matt would decide what to name the little boy they already considered their own.

"I said, I can't do this. I'm sorry. I thought I could, but now I realize that it's just not possible. Last night was the worst night of my life, maybe even worse than the night Brad died. I went down to the nursery to see the baby, and I knew then that somehow I would have to find a way to raise him myself."

Chris's anger quickly overcame her disappointment. The last time she had been forced to deal with her sorrow on her own, the birth mother was long gone, and Matt had tuned her out completely, preferring silence, choosing to keep his thoughts to himself. She thought that she had formed a good relationship with this girl, that they had come to an understanding. Now her trust had been betrayed, leaving her, and most likely her marriage, in shambles.

She took a deep breath, trying to hold back the venom she wanted to spew out at this girl. "Kerry, I'm sure these second thoughts are something all new mothers go through. The counselors mentioned it to us, and I know you and Elaine spoke about it too. But you have promised your baby to us, and I hope these feelings of indecision will pass quickly so that we can keep our date this afternoon. Everything is set for two o'clock, and I hope very much that it will all go as planned."

"Don't speak to me in that condescending tone, Chris. I've heard plenty about these feelings, but now I know first-hand how it feels. You know nothing about this. Of course we all talked about how I would feel, but no one said that it would be like having my guts ripped out. And that's exactly what it feels like. You have no idea, and you never will."

These words wounded Chris the most, and her anger dissolved into tears. "I can't believe you're doing this to us. You promised," she cried.

"It's a promise I can't keep. I'm sorry, I really am. But it's just the way it is. Now I have to talk to Lisbeth, which is what I was starting to do when you came in. Please let me finish. I need to contact everyone and call off this meeting."

"Kerry, think about this, please, I beg you, don't do this to us."

"Please go. Staying won't make me change my mind," Kerry said, reaching for the phone.

Chris stood outside the room, paralyzed with fear. Nothing she'd ever experienced even came close. As bad as last time had been, it didn't compare to this. She had trusted Kerry, and now it was over. Matt had never been totally on board, he had merely given in to her demands. And he had said on numerous occasions that he didn't think their marriage could survive another disappointment as profound as this; she feared that he might be right. What was worse, his plane had probably already landed, and right after he dropped his bags at the office he would be on his way here.

"I'll wait for you at the hospital with our new son in my arms," she had told him. She had been so sure, so optimistic, so naive. What a nightmare this had all become.

She couldn't think straight. Should she stay here and wait for him, or try to head him off at the office? No matter where it took place the confrontation was going to be horrible. Then it occurred to her that Lisbeth would come rushing down here as soon as Kerry called her. Lisbeth was in favor of her and Matt's having the baby, she always had been. Chris would wait right here in the corridor until she arrived. Maybe she could talk some sense into her granddaughter.

Kerry had been able to reach everyone involved in the adoption except Mike Salter, Chris and Matt's attorney. She'd left a message with his secretary. She felt much better having completed the calls, and rewarded herself with a short nap. But she awakened just a few minutes later when she sensed someone standing by her bedside. Mike Salter was staring down at her.

"You startled me," she said, sitting up in bed. She wondered how long he had been there. He was tall and lanky, and his angular features reflected his cold personality. She had disliked him from the moment she'd first laid eyes on him.

"I didn't intend to," he said, in a hard, calculating voice. She knew immediately that he had received her message and had chosen to ignore it. He didn't impress Kerry as a man who liked to lose, and he had come here specifically to avoid having to tell his client that the deal, as Kerry was certain he referred to all his cases, was off.

"I left a message for you at your office. I've canceled our meeting. I've changed my mind," she said.

"I was out," he said, continuing to stare at her. But he hadn't been out at all. When his secretary had told him who was on the line he had bolted from his desk and put on his coat. After years in practice he knew almost for certain that a call from the birth mother was not good news. His instincts proved him right once again. Now she had confirmed his suspicions.

"Well, I'm sorry you were out, and that your secretary wasn't able to give you my message. It would have saved you a trip over here."

He turned and pulled up the visitor's chair that had been pushed against the wall. He put the flowers on the floor and sat down.

"Now Kerry, why don't we start from the beginning, so that I am better able to understand what's going on here."

"I don't know if that would really help," Kerry said. "I thought I had made the right decision, but now I realize that I've made a terrible mistake. I can't give my baby away to Chris and Matt."

"I see," he answered cautiously. "You have decided that you are going to take care of this child and raise it on your own?"

"Yes, that's right, Mr. Salter. It's my baby." She tried to keep her voice from breaking. She would not allow herself to be intimidated by this man. Nothing he could say was going to make her change her mind. Nothing.

"Kerry, didn't you sit in my office just a few weeks ago and tell me, and Chris and Matt, how happy you were that they were going to adopt your baby? How you were sure that they would be good parents and that you were one hundred and ten percent certain, I think you said, that you were making the right decision? Am I mistaken? Wasn't it you who said those things?"

"Yes, of course it was me. But things have changed. Once I saw the baby I knew I could never give him up."

"Kerry, it doesn't seem to me that you have taken this matter very seriously. After all, you promised to give the baby to Chris and Matt. Were you lying when you said those things? Was this all just a big game to you?"

Kerry raised herself up in the bed. She was so angry she could barely speak. Who was this awful man to come and accuse her of lying about something so important? He was horrible, and it seemed to her that he would stop at nothing to get what he wanted. She tried to maintain her composure. She thought back to her sessions with Elaine, and remembered her saying that no one, especially not someone campaigning for the adoptive parents, could convince her to sign the release papers. If that happened, they would be meaningless.

"Mr. Salter, I wasn't lying. At the time I thought it was the right thing to do. Now that I've had the baby, I would be even sorrier if I went ahead with something that I know is wrong. He's my baby, and I am going to keep him."

"So you were lying then. You gave your word and now you're taking it back. I call that a lie."

"Call it whatever you want, but that's the way it is. I'm sorry. Now I'm very tired, please let me rest. This has been very hard for me."

"Oh, I'll bet it has, young lady. It's not every day that

you can destroy people's lives and play games like this. You're going to regret this, I promise you that."

That was it. She had heard enough. "Get out!" she screamed. "You get out of this room right now, or I'll call the nurse and tell her to have you removed. You can't come in here like this and accuse me of playing games and of being a liar. I don't have to listen to this. I'm sorry for what has happened, but I just can't help it!" Nor could she help the tears that streamed down her face, and her uncontrollable sobs.

This was exactly what Mike Salter had been hoping for. Finally she had broken down. The sound of her crying pleased him, for at last he had reached her. He sat back in the chair and continued to stare at her.

"Kerry, I'm sorry to have upset you. But you must realize what you have done is very wrong. You owe it to yourself to go ahead with this, and you owe it to Chris and Matt. Now I've brought the papers for you to sign. We can ask the nurse to come in and witness your signing them. Then the worst will be over, and you can get on with your life. Now what do you say?" He made a move toward his briefcase, certain that he had shamed Kerry into going ahead with the adoption.

"Don't tell me what I owe Chris and Matt. I don't owe them anything. The only person I owe is my baby, and that's all I am concerned about."

The strength of Kerry's voice startled him, and he stopped fishing in his briefcase and looked up at her. For the first time, he saw a strength and determination in her eyes that matched his own. He knew in that instant that he had lost this particular battle. He stood up to go.

"Have a good day, Kerry. Just give it some more thought, that's all I ask," he said as he left.

"This is certainly not what we planned," Lisbeth said, rather sternly. It was a tone of voice Kerry was not used to hearing from her grandmother and she was not prepared for it. She had hoped for more understanding from her, especially after what she had been through with the lawyer. "We all agreed in advance that this was going to be upsetting, and that the first few days were going to be very difficult, but we never considered that you would change your mind like this. You must think once more about the practical considerations of what you are saying. You are not in a position to raise this child."

Kerry did not respond. She just sat in the bed shaking her head. How could Lisbeth turn against her?

"Now," Lisbeth continued, "I can see that you haven't even been out of bed to shower. So, before you put on this new robe I have brought you, that is exactly what you are going to do," she said, pulling back the covers, urging her granddaughter out of bed. "Once you've washed your hair, you're going to feel a great deal better. Then you and I are going to take a long walk around the hospital, and discuss this further. Now up you go."

As she listened to the running water, Lisbeth couldn't

help thinking that she was far too old for this kind of emotional exhaustion. She understood perfectly what Kerry was going through, but that was no reason to allow her to throw her life away. Unfortunately, she seemed adamant about not signing the release papers.

Chris had met her earlier and they'd discussed the problem.

"Elaine's coming to see her this afternoon," Lisbeth had told Chris. "But we can't count on her to convince her one way or another. Her position has always been one of neutrality, and I imagine she will support whatever decision Kerry makes."

"I'm still not giving up hope," Chris insisted. "I made Mike promise not to mention a word to Matt until the decision is absolutely final. He says to give her another day. Maybe she'll change her mind again. I don't want to say a thing to Matt until we know for certain. Thankfully, he has to go to a dinner tonight, a long-standing engagement that he can't cancel, and when he comes home I'm not going to tell him a thing about what happened today. My plan is to lie awake all night and pray that the news will be better in the morning."

"I hope so too, dear. If I hear anything I'll let you know. Keep your fingers crossed," Lisbeth had said before going to see Kerry.

Matt bought the excuse she had concocted, and even though Chris felt terrible about lying to him, she wanted to protect him for as long as possible.

"I'm sure these meetings are changed all the time, for

one reason or another. They involve so many people, it's tough to get everyone together at the same time."

"Right," he said, sounding distracted as he often did when he was in the office.

"That's exactly what happened," she said, a little too quickly. "They'll call with a new time, probably tomorrow morning."

"You'll let me know. But everything else is fine, Kerry is doing well?"

"Oh yes, she's great. A little tired, but that's to be expected."

"Good. This thing tonight could go on for a while, so don't wait up, I'm sure you're tired."

She breathed a sigh of relief. At least one of her prayers had been answered and if her luck held she wouldn't have to face him until morning.

Chapter 21

"Have you heard anything?" Chris asked anxiously. She had held off calling Lisbeth until now, but already it was half past ten and she knew that Lisbeth would say good night to Charles and go off to bed herself.

"Not a word, dear, I'm sorry to report. But I've found that more than anyone I've ever known, Kerry needs her space, and time to consider things all by herself. Let's hope she's using this time to come to her senses. Now try and get some rest, you've been through the mill."

"Truer words . . ." Chris said. "Thanks for everything, Lisbeth. You have been wonderful."

"Not at all, I'm just hoping the morning will bring us better news. Good night, dear."

Chris was so sound asleep that when she first heard the ringing sound she couldn't decide if it was the phone, or if Matt had locked himself out of the apartment. Then she groped for the telephone, afraid that at this hour it could only be bad news.

"Hello," she said, sounding more awake than she really was.

"It's Kerry. I'm so sorry, Chris. I've decided to keep my promise to you. I don't know what happened to me, but it was terrible, and I can only hope that you'll be able to forgive me. I'm especially sorry for the cruel things I said to you. I'll sign the papers in the morning, as soon as we can get everyone together again. But I didn't want to wait until the morning to tell you. Please forgive me, and promise that you'll take good care of my son."

Chris was afraid to speak, afraid that it was a dream. But she held the phone tight, switched on the bedside lamp, and sat straight up in bed.

"Kerry, I hope this is not some kind of game. Are you sure?"

Kerry sounded exhausted, as if she had been crying so hard she had dried out her throat completely. "This is not a game, and I mean what I'm saying. I spent the entire day in the nursery, holding the baby, talking to him, just being close. When they closed up, they made me come back to my room. Only then was I able to think clearly. I guess I just needed some time alone with him, some time when the pressure was off and I could deal with my emotions while I held him in my arms. Elaine warned me that everyone has to find their own way to say good-bye. And this was mine. I'm just sorry I had to put you through all of this. How did Matt take the news? I'll bet that wasn't pretty."

Chris couldn't bring herself to explain all of the antics she had gone through to hide Kerry's change of heart from him. Someday in the future maybe they would be able to laugh about it.

"He'll be fine," she assured her. "I'm so glad you called, Kerry. Now get some sleep. Tomorrow's going to be a big day. Are you sure you are ready to go ahead with this? I don't think I could stand another day like this one. It's been the most painful of my life."

"I know, it has been awful for me too. But now I'm sure," she said. "Now I'm prepared for it."

The process took a little over an hour. Not once did Kerry look directly at Mike Salter. She didn't want to give him the satisfaction of thinking for one moment that he had

had anything to do with her decision to go ahead with the adoption. If anyone had influenced her it had been Lisbeth. She was the person Kerry trusted above all. When she'd seen the pain in her grandmother's eyes as they'd walked slowly through the hospital corridors, she'd suddenly realized that she was making a mistake. "Please don't do this to yourself, Kerry," Lisbeth had said. "You have no idea what a hard road you will be choosing. Let him go, and be happy that he is going to such a good home. Then go forward. There is so much to life that you will miss if you tie yourself down with a baby right now." Those were the words of loving advice that Kerry had taken to heart.

Now she sat up straighter in her chair, as Mike asked her the questions she had read over and over again during the past few months.

"Do you understand that if you change your mind after you sign the consent to adoption, but before the adoption is granted, you must write to the superior court to ask that your consent be withdrawn?"

Matt shifted nervously in his chair, but Chris reached over and took his hand.

"I do," Kerry said without hesitation.

"Do you understand that once the adoption is granted in court, it means the following: you will no longer be responsible for your child."

"Yes, sir."

"The petitioners, Christine and Matthew Brooks, will be responsible for the child."

"Yes, sir."

"Do you understand that at any time you will be able to add information to the agency's adoption record that can be made available to your child? This is especially important for medical records that might be beneficial to the child."

"Yes, I do."

The questions seemed endless and repetitive, but eventually they had all been asked, and the papers were presented for signature.

Kerry signed quickly, then pushed the papers away.

Chris's hand shook as she signed the document, which authorized her to take "Baby Brooks" out of the hospital.

Still, the silence was unbearable when it was time for them to leave.

"Thank you, Kerry," Matt and Chris managed to say. Chris reached out and took Kerry in her arms.

"Take good care of him," was all Kerry could say before she turned and was embraced by Lisbeth.

Chris and Matt headed down the hallway to claim their son.

Lisbeth waited until she could no longer hear their footsteps in the corridor. She had made Chris a promise to make certain that their car was gone from the hospital entrance before they left.

"Let's get you home, dear. King is waiting outside for us," she said, guiding Kerry slowly out of the room, leading her in the direction of her new life.

PART
VI

Chapter 22

Kerry discovered that *Gardens & Homes* was a fun place to work. Its offices were on half of a floor in an old building on Sacramento Street. While the space was far from elegant, it consisted of a series of cubicles constructed out of flimsy partitions; the atmosphere of the office was informal, friendly, and exciting. Only Gretchen had an office with real walls. But she was rarely in it, preferring to hold impromptu meetings in the passageways and to dash in and out of the cubicles, checking on photos, copy, and advertising. One of the great benefits of working for Gretchen, Kerry soon learned, was that she gave as much consideration to a suggestion made by a research assistant as to one offered by the art director. All she wanted was what was best for the magazine. Gretchen had hand-picked every one of her hardworking staff of eight, and the casual environment belied the long hours and team effort that had made the magazine such a success.

Since the staff was so small, everyone learned very quickly that they would be called upon to do whatever was required to get the best material, and to meet the monthly deadlines. Gretchen had no tolerance for egos.

Kerry was assigned a small space that she could call her

own, and word spread quickly that the new girl was both smart and ambitious, and could be counted on to do a thorough job, no matter what the task. She also did it with a smile, and her attitude went a long way in getting busy, stressed-out people to stop what they were doing and help her when she needed it.

Most of all the job gave Kerry a place to go every morning, a place where she was expected and had responsibilities. From the moment she walked through the door every second was occupied, and she didn't have a chance to think about anything else. It provided her with an escape from her thoughts about the baby. She couldn't afford to sit around all day and think about what could have been. Still, the nights were the worst; she would lie awake in bed and dream of holding her little boy. She joined a gym and started going every night after work, not only to get rid of the few excess pounds that she just couldn't shake, but also to exhaust herself so she could fall asleep more easily.

She had done so well at the magazine that in the middle of November, when one of the copy assistants left, Gretchen offered her the job.

"Wow, do you really mean it?"

"You should know by now I never joke about things like this. I take this magazine very seriously, and I know you'll be terrific in this position. I do have one major concern, but we'll have to work around it. What are your plans for school?"

"I had planned to start in January, but I could postpone—"

"Not on your life, young lady, you're not giving up a formal education for this. As good as it is, it is no replacement for college. First, your grandmother would never forgive me, and second, it wouldn't be in your best interests. No, we'll just have to work around it. But it will be at the risk of having a great social life, I'm afraid."

"That's fine with me," Kerry agreed at once.

"By the way, I hope you're making some new friends now that you're on your own."

She hadn't really. She had some acquaintances at the gym, but she never saw them at other times. Most of her new friends were several young people in the office.

"Well, kind of," she began. "Everyone here has been very nice. In fact, they've invited me to what they're calling an orphan party. It's for all of us who aren't going to be with our families at Thanksgiving. I don't have plans to go home until Christmas, so I'll be around. But we're doing it a week before the real Thanksgiving so we can include those who won't be here as well. It's just an excuse for a party."

"I'm glad to hear it, even happier that it's not on the real holiday, because I was hoping you could come up to our house for Thanksgiving. I've already asked Lisbeth, and she thinks Charles might be able to make it also. Now that they're neighbors, it won't be such an arduous outing for him."

Gretchen was referring to the house Lisbeth had rented in the little town of Rutherford, just a few miles from her home in the Napa Valley.

Lisbeth hadn't said so, but Kerry suspected that one of

the reasons she'd taken the house was to give Kerry a place where she could spend time with her. She hadn't been to the house in Pacific Heights since the night she'd left for the hospital to deliver the baby. She was thrilled that her grandmother had rented the country house and looked forward to going there as often as possible.

"I'd love to go to your place for Thanksgiving, Gretchen. In fact there's no place I'd rather be."

"I'll plan on it then, and I know Josh will be happy to see you too. He's always asking how you're doing."

Kerry hadn't counted on that, but now that she was no longer forced to hide behind a sweater, she might just take him up on his offer of a horseback ride through the vineyards.

"You seem different, somehow," Josh said to Kerry as he took a plate from her. They had drawn dish duty because Gretchen had given the help Thanksgiving night off.

"In what way?" she asked curiously.

He smiled over at her, and accepted another plate. "I can't quite tell what it is. First of all, you look terrific. Last time you were all bundled up in that sweater, even on a hot day. I thought maybe you were coming down with the flu or something. And I don't know, you seemed, somehow nervous, or worried about something. Distant is maybe the best way to describe it. The only time I saw you smile that day was when you were playing with the dogs."

So he had noticed, she thought. He was more observant than she had given him credit for.

"I'm shy around people I don't know very well," she said. "So that day was kind of difficult for me. And then I felt I really didn't have much to add to the conversation. I haven't even finished college yet, and law school is a totally foreign world to me."

"Boy did we ever talk about that a lot. I felt badly after you left. I apologize, it was a bit much. It's just that it was right before school started, and we were all so excited to have been accepted in the first place. You were probably glad to get out of here."

"Not at all," she lied. "I found it all very interesting."

"You're lying," he said with a laugh. "I think that obnoxious lunchtime conversation is why you didn't want to have anything to do with me when I called you and asked you to go riding. You were afraid that I'd take you out and talk about nothing but torts. Is that right?"

She giggled, thinking back to that day, and how she'd imagined her very pregnant self perched on a horse. "No, that wasn't it at all."

"Just don't like me period, is that it?"

But she did like him, she realized, and this conversation had cleared up many of the misconcpetions she'd had about him. Now instead of finding him self-centered and spoiled, she found him to be a really caring guy. His sense of humor, especially about himself, was very appealing. His looks had never been in question. He was as handsome as anyone she had ever met, and now she was learning that his personality might be just as winsome as his appearance.

"Don't be silly," she teased. "And hurry up, all this talking is slowing down the process." She turned back to the sink so that he wouldn't see that she was blushing.

"If that's the case, how about a ride tomorrow? It's supposed to be beautiful. And if I become impossible out there, Betsy and Igor will show you the way home."

"I'd like that," she answered.

"Deal. I'll pick you up around nine, and then we can have lunch back here. Mom and Dad are going to visit some friends, so with the help off, we might want to go into town."

"Or maybe when you come by we can pick something up from the store in town. Then we won't have to go all the way back," she suggested, having heard from his mother that Josh rarely entered a kitchen.

"Smart girl," he said, hanging up the dish towel on the rack near the stove.

The day was perfect for riding, and even though Kerry knew she was going to be terribly sore on Saturday, they rode full out until late in the afternoon.

"Let's not stop for lunch, we can eat later if we're hungry," Kerry said. "I'm having too much fun. This is the prettiest country I have ever seen. That all right with you?"

"Fine with me," Josh agreed. "Carry on." And he led them up into the hills. At the top of the crest they stopped and admired the view of the entire Napa Valley below. Betsy and Igor stayed with them all the way. "These are going to be two tired little doggies tonight," he said of them.

"I have the feeling I will be too," Kerry added. "But it's well worth it."

When they finally returned to the barn it was nearly dark. As Josh reached up to help Kerry take her saddle off the big mare she had been riding, his hand brushed hers. Kerry jumped.

"Wow, I'm sorry, did I scare you or something?"

She tried to hide her embarrassment of having overreacted. "No, I'm sorry, I thought the saddle was going to fall."

They walked back to the house together, only to find that Gretchen and Jack hadn't returned yet. They went straight to the kitchen and searched the refrigerator like scavengers.

"I'm ravenous," Josh said, taking a bite out of a cold turkey leg, and then offering it to her. She found this to be a very sexy gesture, and she smiled before sinking her teeth into it.

They peeled back the foil covers on more Thanksgiving leftovers and stood with the refrigerator door open, spooning out scoops of cold mashed potatoes, yams, even Brussels sprouts. Then they took turns finishing off a pumpkin pie directly from the tin.

"Good thing my mom isn't here, she'd kill us. Correction, she'd kill me, for being such a slob. I've tried to explain to her that sometimes food tastes better right out of the carton, but she doesn't seem to get it. She'd have a tough time in law school since four out of five meals come directly out of those white-paper Chinese take-out cartons. After a while it all tastes the same."

Kerry laughed, startled by the sound of her own laughter. It had been a very long time since she'd felt like laughing.

When Josh told her that he had to go back to the city that night, to study for exams, she was amazed at how deeply disappointed she felt.

"I would like to see you in town, very much," he added.

"Me too, and I can't thank you enough for this wonderful day."

"I'll call you just as soon as exams are over. We'll make plans."

"I'd like that," she said, smiling and thinking what a difference a weekend could make.

Chapter 23

The merchants in San Francisco went all out during the holiday season. The stores lining Geary and Post streets competed for the best Christmas decorations, and the result was that each one was more creative and festive than the next.

Kerry dashed out of the office every day at lunch, caught the cable car up California Street and then down Powell to Union Square to do her shopping. It made her feel good to walk in and out of the shops, buying presents for everyone with money she had earned herself.

But what she enjoyed most was selecting gifts for the baby. She bought toys, (even though Lisbeth had reported that he had every type of toy imaginable), clothes, and even some books that Chris could save for later. When she got all the packages back to the apartment she wrapped each one individually and wrote a card for every single one.

She still had trouble with his name, for the Brookses had decided to call him Shelby. She had hated the name when she'd first heard it, and she hadn't learned to like it any better during the past four months.

When she and Brad had talked about naming their children, they had always agreed that if it was a girl they would name her Jennifer. Brad was partial to the name Ben for a boy, but she had insisted that their son be named after his father. Now she felt a sense of panic because she couldn't even remember the other names they had considered. Memories of things that used to be so important to her were slowly fading away.

Chris had called her two weeks earlier. "Kerry, I just want you to know that if you want to see the baby, you are more than welcome to come over. We'll be leaving for Chicago on the twentieth, we're going to spend the holidays with Matt's parents and we won't be back until the fifth of January. Shelby's doing so well, and growing like a weed."

"You're sweet to call. If you hadn't I was going to call you next week, because I do want to come over. For the first time I feel strong enough to handle it. Plus, I have many bags of presents for him." The last time she had seen him he was only two days old.

"Great, I'll look forward to it, you just let me know when."

Kerry had circled the date on her calendar, thinking then that it was ages away, but now it was time to load all the packages in a taxi and make the trip up the hill to visit Shelby.

"Big butterflies, big, big ones," she said when Chris opened the door.

"Me too," Chris agreed, taking the bags from Kerry and holding open her arms to her.

"You look terrific! Boy, I didn't know you had such a small waist," she said, admiring her figure.

"It's coming along. Many, many miles on the treadmill, and countless containers of low-fat cottage cheese. Not very tasty, but it works."

"It sure does."

"So, where is he?" Kerry asked, all of a sudden feeling very uncomfortable.

"Still sleeping, I'm afraid, but that will change any minute. Follow me and we'll see what he's up to."

The nursery looked like it was right out of a magazine. Colorful dancing bears had been stenciled around the perimeter of the room. The floor was barely visible because of all the stuffed animals and toys. One wall contained the beginnings of a library. In the corner was a big crib, with a blue and white comforter covering a little sleeping form.

Chris took Kerry's hand and led her over to the crib. Kerry looked in slowly and saw her darling little boy. He was sleeping soundly. It was so still in the room that she could hear the soft breathing noise he made.

"Let's not wake him," she said, thinking that if she could go now it wouldn't be so difficult to leave.

"Don't be ridiculous, it's not as if you come up here every day," Chris answered. "Go ahead, pick him up. I'll be standing by with a bottle."

Kerry reached into the crib and lifted the little body to her chest. The first thing she noticed was his sweet smell, fresh and innocent. It was exactly as she remembered it from the nursery. She held him up against her, and slowly he awakened, pulling his head back to look at the intruder who had disturbed his sleep. She looked down into his eyes, the eyes of his father. It was Brad gazing up at her. She gently pushed his head back against her, and sat down in the rocking chair at the side of the crib.

She rocked him back and forth, treasuring the feeling of his tiny body against hers. Then slowly the cries came, and as promised, Chris handed her a bottle.

Kerry hesitated. "Go ahead," Chris encouraged her. "There's no magic to it. He knows exactly what to do with it. Just hold it up high enough so that he doesn't get a lot of air with the formula."

"All right," Kerry agreed, guiding the nipple slowly

into his mouth. He pulled at it eagerly, and suddenly she regretted that she had never been able to give him nourishment from her own body, never felt his tiny lips suckling her own breasts.

He took the bottle for a few minutes, and when he had enough, he pushed it out. She held him up and burped him and soon he fell right back to sleep.

"Well, that's about it at this age," Chris said. "He eats, sleeps, cries, has a diaper change, burps, sleeps. It's a pretty simple life so far, but it sure keeps me busy."

They sat in silence for a few more minutes, and then Kerry felt that she should go. There was really nothing more to say.

"Have a wonderful time in Chicago," she offered.

"Thank you. It will be fun to see everyone, especially since they haven't had a chance to see their new grandson."

Chris's words irritated Kerry. What a charade, she thought.

"Lisbeth tells me that your family is coming here and that you're all going to celebrate Christmas up in Rutherford. That sounds good."

"Yes, it will be, I'm looking forward to it." But it won't be complete, it will seem empty and pointless, not having my baby there, she wanted to add but didn't dare.

"Please come back soon after New Year's if you feel like it," Chris said. "You know you're always welcome. And thanks for all the presents. Oh, I almost forgot," she said, disappearing for a moment down the hallway. "Here are some pictures I wanted you to have. We took them on his three-month birthday." Kerry took the photos without looking at them and put them in her jacket pocket.

I am the mother of that beautiful baby who is sleeping in there, she wanted to scream out. But she merely wished Chris a happy Christmas and walked quickly away from the house.

Chapter 24

The house in Rutherford was a big Victorian, with six bedrooms, two living rooms, and countless nooks that invited its guests to curl up with a book. Even with all of them staying there—Lisbeth, Charles, King, Mary, Nancy, Coach, Willy, and Kerry—it didn't feel crowded at all.

"I had to search all over for you," Nancy said, discovering Kerry curled up in a window seat in an upstairs room at the end of the hall. She was busy reviewing an article on bulbs for next month's issue. "What an odd little space. What do you think it was used for?"

"I have no idea, but I love it. It's very cozy. I've been up here most of the afternoon, and I'm almost finished with my work."

"That's good to hear. I hope I'm not disturbing you."

Kerry was glad to see her mother and she put her papers down and shifted over on the narrow banquette to make room for her to sit down.

She patted the chintz cushion. "Not one bit. Sit."

"You're really enjoying your job, aren't you? From your letters I feel as if I know some of the people you work with."

Kerry wrote home at least twice a week. She looked at it as a good way to practice her writing, as well as a way of trying to open up the lines of communication with her family again. She wrote so much about work because she couldn't mention the most important thing in her life; her feelings about her baby. Neither her father nor her brother even knew he existed. She had mentioned Josh once or twice, and she looked forward to introducing him to her family.

"For a first job I sure lucked out. I love it. The staff is great and Gretchen has been the best. And Josh has become a good friend. As I told you in my letters, at first I couldn't stand him, but I don't think I've ever been so wrong about anyone. I think you'll like him."

"I'm happy for you. But I really came up here looking for you because your father and brother have gone into town for a few hours. I wanted to talk with you and find out how you are really doing."

Kerry was happy that her mother was making the effort, but still couldn't understand why she just couldn't come out and ask what she really wanted to know. "That's nice, Mom. You mean you want to know about the baby?"

"Yes, I do."

"Well, he's fine. They named him Shelby, which I'm not crazy about. In fact, I hate it. And I'm glad Brad will never know because he would have a fit. Isn't it an awful name?"

"Wouldn't have been anywhere near the top of my list," Nancy agreed. "But how is he—is he healthy?"

"Very, and growing like a weed. I went to see him for the first time last week."

Nancy stiffened. "Kerry, your keeping in contact with these people is only going to make things harder for you. Cards and letters are one thing, but face-to-face meetings?"

Kerry nodded. "It was painful, much harder than I thought it would be. I bought him some Christmas presents, and instead of just sending them over, I thought it would be nice if I went to the house, to see Chris and, of course, the baby. So that's what I did. I held him and fed him his bottle. It was very difficult leaving without him, and I think about him now much more than I did before."

"Surely you're not thinking about changing your mind?"

"I wish I could, but I have to think about what a nice home Chris and Matt have made for him. You should see his nursery. It's decorated with wallpaper that has dancing bears on it, and there are toys and books everywhere. I have to believe that they are going to be very good parents. But to tell the truth, focusing on that aspect doesn't make it any easier."

"I can imagine how painful it is, but you're being very mature about it. Try to keep thinking that way, and in time the hurt will lessen."

"I will, Mom, but somehow I think that this is one thing time will not heal. I expect to carry this empty feeling with me for the rest of my life. For as long as I live, there will always be a part of me that will long for the baby I couldn't keep."

Nancy gave her a sympathetic smile. "That may be, but I want you to know how proud I am of how you are handling it. You really are much more like Lisbeth's own daughter than I am. Her strong character seems to have skipped a generation."

"We all have our pluses and minuses, Mom. My ability to deal with major problems was pushed to the limit this year. Lisbeth taught me a thing or two about how to deal with adversity in life. She's one of a kind."

"She is at that, and in an odd way, the fact that you turned to her for help has improved our relationship too. So you see, some good did come out of this." Nancy smiled, then she leaned over and kissed her daughter on the cheek.

"I'm glad to have you back in my life. Finish up and then come downstairs and sit by the fire. Your dad will be back soon, and he's missed you more than you will ever know."

It was two full days until Josh would arrive. Even though Kerry was busy spending time with Coach and Willy, running into town to pick up last-minute gifts, she thought about him frequently.

They had been seeing each other at least four nights a week ever since Thanksgiving, and rarely did a day pass when they didn't speak to each other. Usually, after Josh was through with classes, and Kerry had finished at the office, they met for dinner and a movie. They had spent one Sunday in Sausalito, admiring the boats and eating hamburgers at an outdoor restaurant. Kerry had never met anyone who was so easy to talk to. But still she hadn't mentioned Brad's death. She felt that she couldn't talk about that without also mentioning the baby. The two issues were inextricably linked in her mind. She was keeping her secret from him.

On the night Josh was supposed to arrive in Napa, he called her shortly after ten.

"I have assembled possibly the best, or worst, depending on your perspective, collection of inane and mindless movies ever made by man. Any chance you want to watch them with me?"

He did make her laugh. "Yes, I would," she answered, "but can we do it over at your house? Everybody here was dead tired tonight, and they've all gone to bed."

"Sure, I'm on my way to pick you up."

His call came at exactly the right time. The house had suddenly become quiet once everyone turned in, and her mind began to travel in the direction she had deemed off limits. Last Christmas had been the happiest time in her life. She had been so sure then that her future was secure, her engagement to Brad only the beginning of much good fortune to come. They would marry and have children. He would fulfill his dream of becoming a doctor, she a writer. But since that night there had been enough heartbreak and disappointment to last her a lifetime. She had thought she had rounded the corner in the grieving process, but then she had gone to visit the baby. Ever since that afternoon, she hadn't been able to stop thinking about the little boy. She knew she still could legally reclaim the child. Her head told her it was wrong even to contemplate this, but her heart ached with the need to have her baby.

When Kerry heard the crunching sound of tires on the gravel driveway, she took her jacket off the hook in the hallway and rushed out to meet Josh. She was very thankful for his company tonight.

At his parents' house, Josh added logs to the fire that was burning in the den. They settled in on the big sofa to watch one of the movies Josh had promised would take "not one iota of brain power to follow." He was right, she thought, as action heroes killed one bad guy after another. As she tuned out the awful dialogue, her own troublesome thoughts drifted through her mind.

"Because we live in inflationary times, I will give you not just a penny, but an entire dollar for your thoughts," he said, but there was no response. He waved his hand in front of her face.

"I am speaking to you, or trying to anyway," he said.

She blinked away her dreams. "Oh sorry, what did you say?"

He shook his head. "I said that due to inflation, I will

give you a dollar for your thoughts. But maybe I have to up the offer. You are right here next to me, but you are a gazillion miles away. If I believed in out-of-body experiences, I would say you might be having one right now."

"How many is a gazillion?" she asked, trying to deflect his attention from her.

"Oh no, Kerry, you're not getting off that easily. I don't understand you. I haven't seen you for five days, and I've missed you, yet you have nothing to say to me. Now what is going on? Is it something about your parents?"

"It's nothing . . . really," Kerry said, uncertain about whether she should tell him what was bothering her.

"Sorry Kerry, I won't accept that as an answer. Every time you go off into one of your distant moods, and I ask you what is wrong, you say nothing. Now, we're either going to be real friends, or we can go our separate ways and stop devoting so much time to a relationship that is going nowhere. I know what direction I would like to take. I'm much too fond of you not to want to try and help if something is bothering you. And the look on your face right now tells me that you are very unhappy."

She knew that it was now or never. She would just have to trust that he would understand.

"This has been a very difficult year for me," she began. "Last year at this time, a year ago to the day, in fact, I got engaged. It was such a happy time, and I was thrilled to be marrying Brad. He was a really terrific guy, we practically grew up together. His family lived in the house right down the street from us, and for ages we were friends, until his sister suggested he stop considering me just the tomboy next door and ask me to go out. From then on we were inseparable, and we planned to get married, have children and careers, the whole package. He was studying at UCLA to be a doctor." She looked over at him and took a deep breath. She wanted to get the entire story out before her emotions took over.

"I know it sounds trite, and it doesn't make it any easier, but these things happen, Kerry. People really think they have a future together, but then something happens that changes all that. I know, it happened to me once."

"Not like this, it didn't," Kerry said, pulling back from his embrace. "Unfortunately that's only the beginning of the story. Brad was killed in a car accident last April. And the worst part of all was that he died before I had a chance to tell him that we were going to have a baby."

"Oh, my God!" was all Josh could manage.

"So now you know everything, well almost, anyway," she said. And for the rest of the night they remained on the sofa, and Kerry took him through the roller-coaster ride that had been the past year. There were many tears and some brief moments of laughter, especially when she told him what she'd been thinking the day he had called her to go riding. "Can you imagine? I probably would have given birth right out there in the vineyards, among the Pinot Noir grapes," she laughed. "I think I went into labor about forty-eight hours after you called."

Her mood saddened again when she talked about her

visit to see the baby, but she stopped short of telling him that she was thinking about trying to take him back.

When the first light of the day before Christmas came over the hillside, they were still taking turns finding out about each other's past.

Josh stood up and stretched, then went to the window and pulled back the curtains. "It's going to be a beautiful day," he said. "If we can stay awake for it. Let's go out for a walk, we'll take the dogs, then I'll drive you home. We both need some rest."

The fresh air was invigorating, and with Betsy and Igor in tow they headed up the path of the house. Kerry could have walked for miles, but Josh was anxious to get some sleep. They stopped near the spot where they had taken the horses at Thanksgiving.

"Kerry, I'm glad we finally got everything out in the open. At least I feel better your not having any secrets from me."

"Me too," she agreed.

Then he took her in his arms and kissed her. At first she didn't hesitate, but as his hands began to explore the back of her neck, her shoulders, and then traveled forward to the top of her breasts, she suddenly pulled away from him.

Brad's face appeared before her, as clear as the morning sky. She couldn't shake the image as Josh's hands continued their path up and down her back. "Stop, please, I can't," she cried, sounding both confused and angry. "I'm sorry, it's not that I don't want to, I . . . oh, I don't know what I feel."

"I'm sorry too. I've wanted to kiss you for so long, I couldn't help myself. I care for you very much, and I'd love to see you happy again."

"You're so sweet," she said, "such a good friend."

"I see this relationship as something more than friendship."

"I know, I do too. But judging from what just happened, I may not be ready for that yet. But I'm willing to try," she offered.

"And I'm willing to wait," he said, "for as long as it takes. I have the feeling you're worth waiting for."

PART
VII

Chapter 25

"Kerry, come down to my office, will you please?" Gretchen said. It was more of a command than a request.

The others within earshot looked up from their desks. Kerry, as well as everyone else in the office, knew that being summoned to Gretchen's office meant either very good or very bad news.

Kerry grabbed a pad and a pen, although she suspected the meeting would require neither one.

"Close the door behind you, if you would," Gretchen said when she appeared in the doorway.

Kerry settled herself opposite the woman who had been her staunchest supporter. "Kerry, sit down. I want to know what's going on. I have here in front of me another article that was supposed to have been fact-checked, proofed, and revised with the author sometime early last week, and I just learned that none of those things have been done. We won't make the issue. This article will not be published as planned and promised. This is not the first time you've slipped up, but the third in the last month. The first two errors I chose to ignore because they weren't as serious as this one and I thought that someone as good as you are deserves the benefit of the doubt, but now your carelessness is hurting the magazine, and I simply will not allow that to happen. What is the matter? Is school and a full-time job too much for you to handle? If that's the case, let's talk about it, and see what can be done."

Kerry had dreaded this moment. Ever since she'd returned from Christmas break, she'd paid little attention to her responsibilities at the magazine. All she'd been able to think about was how she was going to get her baby back. Just this week she had taken the first step toward reclaiming him. She knew that the turmoil in her personal life was affecting the quality of her work and she felt terrible about having let Gretchen down.

"Gretchen, I'm really sorry. But everything is okay now, and I'm back here one hundred percent. I promise. School is fine. I'm managing all the classes without a problem. I'm sorry I've acted so irresponsibly. Please let me have another chance. It won't happen again."

She needed this job more than ever, now that she had to prove to the court that she was able to provide for the baby. She held her breath and awaited Gretchen's answer.

"All right, we'll start over again. But one hundred percent isn't going to do it. You've eroded my trust in you. That's not to say that it can't be earned back, but it's going to take a superhuman effort to do so. And right now we need everyone to perform at superhuman levels. I can't afford any more mistakes like this one. Do we understand each other?"

"Thank you, and yes, I understand perfectly well."

"Good, now march yourself right back to your desk and get to work."

She was almost in the hallway when Gretchen spoke again. "Kerry, one more thing. We saw Josh last night for dinner. He asked about you, so I assume you haven't seen him for a while. I hope none of this had anything to do with him."

"Not to worry, it didn't at all. He's a great guy. I've just been busy with some other things—you know, school and all."

The expression on Gretchen's face told her she didn't believe her for one second.

Josh. How she missed their evenings together, and the times when they laughed, and ate, and talked about things other than her baby. After New Year's Eve, which they had celebrated with his law school friends, Allison and Donny, she had told him that she felt she needed some time alone to sort out her feelings. The physical part of their relationship had not progressed. She longed to see him, or talk to him on the phone, but she didn't dare make the first move because she feared that he would take it to mean that she was ready to be with him in the way he wanted. She wished she could be, but not until she had solved the problem that weighed constantly on her mind. She would get the baby back, and adjust to a new life with her son. And then she would see if she had any energy left over to devote to their relationship.

She had started the process of reclaiming her son by writing a letter, which had to be filed with the clerk of the Superior Court. She had spent the past two nights writing and rewriting the letter, in the hope of convincing the judge that she was worthy of having her baby back. "I made the decision to let the baby be adopted well before he was born, before I had the chance to see him and hold him," she began. "I was scared and afraid that I would be unable to care for him as I knew I would want him to be cared for. I wanted the world for him, and thought that it would be better if he went to a home where he had two parents who would love him and care for him. I was wrong. I was totally unprepared for the depth of my feelings for my son. They are unlike anything I have ever experienced before. I was overwhelmed by the love and affection I felt for him from the very first moment I saw him. In fact, I had decided not to go forward with the adoption when I was still in the hospital, but family members and the lawyer representing the adoptive parents were very tough on me, and encouraged me to change my mind back again. But now that I have had time to think about it, I know that my first instincts were correct, and that the baby belongs with me. He is constantly in my thoughts. I am sure that one birth parent is better than two people who are totally unrelated to him can ever be. No matter how much they claim to love him. Since giving birth, I have found a good job with a secure future. I now have my own apartment, which has more than enough room for the two of us. I hope you will consider my request, and will rule in my favor. I am the child's mother, and I feel there is no better place in the world for my son than with me. Thank you for your consideration." She hoped the letter sounded as heartfelt as it was. Now it was up to the judge to hear all sides of the story and then to rule.

• • •

Kerry had no idea where the Superior Court was located, but she assumed it was somewhere downtown in the middle of the buildings that housed all the other state offices. She would find out soon enough, for she had the letter tucked safely in her backpack, and she planned to take it down today on her lunch hour. After her meeting with Gretchen she was hesitant to go out at all, but she had to deliver the papers.

When Kerry entered the imposing building, she found the main floor bustling with people scurrying in every direction. She searched for someone to give her directions to the Superior Court. She was standing in the center of the rotunda looking around frantically, aware that precious time was passing, when she saw him. Only his back was visible, but she recognized the curly hair and familiar leather jacket. He was talking to a girl dressed in jeans and a navy blazer. The woman faced her and Kerry could see that she was pretty, very pretty, with long dark hair. She was carrying a big portfolio stuffed with papers. Her eyes sparkled as they spoke, and then suddenly, before Kerry could get out of their way, they turned and were heading right toward her.

"Kerry," Josh yelled above the noise. He hurried toward her. "Hi, what are you doing here? Don't tell me Mom's gone off the deep end and has sent you to interview judges about their gardens."

Kerry was so concerned about delivering her letter that

she couldn't even force a smile. "Hi," she said, despite everything feeling awfully happy to see him. "No, it's nothing like that. I'm here for my own stuff. Besides, right now I'm not getting any assignments. I'm busy trying to work myself back into your mother's good graces. I'm in terrible trouble with her," she added.

"Why's that? You must be exaggerating. You're her favorite."

"Well, it's a long story. Maybe I'll tell you sometime. But right now I need to find the Superior Court. Do you know where it is?"

"Yes, I do happen to know. You're in luck, I know this building like the back of my hand. I'm headed in that direction myself. But just to pick up a file for class. Do you have time for a cup of coffee?"

She remembered fondly the hours they had lingered over a single espresso. "Well, okay," she hesitated, thinking of a pile of work on her desk, "but a quick one. I really have to get back."

"Promise, I've got my car so I'll drop you off at the office. That will save some time."

"What about your friend?" she asked, gesturing toward the pretty girl who had stopped to talk with someone else.

"Oh, you mean Rebecca? I'll tell her I'll see her later."

He seemed to read her thoughts. "She's only a classmate, Kerry. Girls go to law school too, you know."

"Don't be snippy," she said.

He led the way to the Superior Court and she handed the letter over to the clerk.

· · ·

"So what brought you down here?" Josh asked as he set down the tray containing their cappuccinos and a croissant they had agreed to share.

The days of being evasive with him were over. He knew her well enough now to know when she was lying, or, at least not telling the whole truth. "I've decided to try to get my baby back. To withdraw my consent to let Chris and Matt adopt him. The first step in doing that is to file a letter with the court, letting them know of my intentions."

"You've decided to do what?" he almost screamed.

She was surprised by how angry he seemed. "Please don't involve the whole restaurant in this. I have decided to take my baby back. The adoption hasn't been granted, and I have every right, according to the law, to ask that he be returned to me."

"Kerry, you have to be kidding." He looked down into his coffee cup and shook his head.

"On the contrary, I've never been more serious or determined about anything in my whole life. Why are you so shocked?"

"I can't believe you're going forward with this. You alluded to it at Christmas, but I thought that after you got back to work, and some more time passed, you'd see that what you did was the right thing. You found a wonderful home for him, and two people who obviously love him very much. You should find peace in that and let it go. And get on with your life."

"He is my life," she shot back. "Don't you see, I feel incomplete without him. I think about him all the time. You have no idea how it is to be consumed with thoughts about your own baby. I feel I've betrayed everyone by doing this—Brad, my family, and especially the baby."

"It's just not right, Kerry. How old is he now anyway, almost six months, right?"

"He was five months old last week."

"That's what I mean. Don't you realize that he has already bonded with Chris and Matt? They are his parents. They have provided a good home for him and they love him. He is part of their lives now. An enormous part. You're just someone who came in and gave him a bottle one afternoon. He doesn't even know you."

Kerry felt like she was fighting an uphill battle, trying to make him understand how she felt. "Josh, you're entitled to your opinion, and you have made it crystal clear what you think about this. But as far as the law is concerned, I am perfectly within my rights to ask for my baby back."

"Screw the law," he shouted, causing others to look over at their table. "There are plenty of statutes on the books that should be changed. And this is certainly one of them. Those laws worked when adoption was a big, deep, dark secret and the records were sealed. Adopted children's identities were kept from them until they were grown up and then some of them embarked on a desperate search to find out where they came from. But no longer. It seems to me that you have the chance here to make the best of this situation.

"Obviously Chris, and to some extent Matt, are willing to make you a part of Shelby's life. You can exchange photos, buy presents for him at holidays and on his birthday, and you can even see him from time to time. And you can always communicate with him through letters and cards. All that should make it easier to live with your decision.

"But you can't just go in there now, five months after he's been with them, and yank this poor baby away from those people. You'll be tearing a family apart, and no one will be the winner. Imagine what Chris and Matt are going to feel when they are served with the letter that you have just obliged the court to send. It will be like a shot through their hearts. And then, if you lose, if the court decides that the baby has been with them for too long, that you are not as prepared to care for him as they are, or any of a number of other reasons, and you are not given custody, I guarantee you that they will petition the court to limit your rights to see the child. And they will probably win. A judge might rule that, because you have this habit of changing your mind over and over again. You already told me how tough their lawyer is. It sounds like this guy will stop at nothing to keep you from getting the baby. He's a pit bull. If you thought he was bad in the hospital, wait until he gets you in the judge's chambers for the hearing. He'll make mincemeat out of you. He'll dig up things from your past even you don't remember. He'll ask you questions that will shock you. And you'll be forced to answer them, and to answer them honestly. It could be the most painful experience of your life. Maybe you should have thought about that before you rushed down here with that letter. And don't forget, even if the judge rules in your favor, Chris and Matt can appeal the decision. A smart lawyer can hold this thing up for many more months, and while the appeal process is going on, the child stays with them."

"They'll never do that," Kerry interjected. "An appeal is the last thing they would consider. Chris would be putting her marriage on the line. Matt wasn't very keen on adopting the baby in the first place. No, he would never agree to that. I know that for sure. Just as I know for sure that this is what I want to do, what I have to do."

"Right now, you think it's what you want, but you're going to cause more heartache than you ever thought possible. If you think it hurts now to be separated from Shelby, wait until you are ordered by law to stay away from him. I would think that seeing him occasionally, having the chance to play with him, and knowing firsthand that he is all right is better than having to rely on letters and reports from Chris. Just because it takes so long in this state for an adoption to be finalized doesn't mean that you should take advantage of it. And just because the law says you can change your mind doesn't make it morally right."

"You know," she began calmly, "the first day I met you I thought that you were a self-centered, highly self-absorbed person. Full of yourself and your fancy law school. I felt the same about all your equally egotistical friends. During lunch I was shocked by how much of the conversation revolved around you; you were only interested in talking about things that related to you. Then you convinced me otherwise. But I should really have more confidence in my first impressions about people. And in my instincts, which told me to keep my baby. From now on I'm going to follow my intuition. It will save me a lot of trouble."

She pushed back her chair and ran out into the street, waving her hand frantically at the passing taxis.

Chapter 26

A decision, once made, was supposed to provide peace of mind, Kerry had always thought. But now she found that wasn't the case at all. It was four in the morning. She'd woken up over an hour ago and couldn't get back to sleep. She couldn't stop thinking about her run-in with Josh. She was still shocked by how jealous she'd felt when she'd seen him with Rebecca. She was coming to realize how strong her feelings for him were. But what disturbed her more than anything, and what was causing her to rethink the whole idea of trying to get her baby back, was Josh's point about her not being able to see her son again if she lost her battle with the Brookses.

She had read the law so many times she had practically memorized it. It stated that the court would always try to keep the best interests of the child in mind. But the Superior Court was required to make a case-by-case analysis. The judge would consider the age of the child (on that point she thought she was okay; when the child was already two or three, the birth mother rarely won), the extent of bonding with the prospective adoptive parents (that was her weakest point; there was no doubt that Chris and Matt had been there since the beginning), and the ability of the natural parents to take care of the child. The law stated that the case would be judged on the demeanor, attitude, intonation, and sincerity of the birth mother. Only after all these things were considered was it possible for the judge to dismiss the adoption proceedings and order Matt and Chris to give the baby back to her.

But what if she lost? Until today, she had never even allowed herself to consider that maybe, just maybe, the court would not rule in her favor. That was unthinkable, the worst possible fate she could imagine. And never for one instant had she considered that Matt and Chris might choose to appeal the decision. Josh had wisely pointed out that it could take months, maybe even a year, for a final decision to be made. And if she didn't win, was she risking never seeing her child again? Was it worth that risk? She tossed and turned and told herself that if she didn't get some rest she would never be able to think clearly, and would find herself in deeper and deeper trouble at the magazine.

She couldn't recall having read any cases in which the birth mother had been denied her right to the baby, and also had been ordered by law to stay away from him. But maybe Josh knew of such cases.

Well, she decided, he brought it up, and he would have to tell her everything he knew about it. Right this very minute. She threw back the covers, pulled on jeans, a T-shirt, and a sweater, and without even bothering to comb her hair, she left the apartment and headed up the hill. Walking quickly she could be at his house in under ten minutes. It was pouring rain, but she didn't bother to turn back for an umbrella. She just pulled her sweater tightly around her and marched on through the torrential downpour.

"Yes, I'm coming," she heard his sleepy voice as he padded down the hallway to the front door. He lived on the ground floor of a large house. The apartment was tiny, but off the back he had a big garden all to himself.

"Kerry, you're soaked," he said, not sounding as surprised as she'd thought he'd be to see her at this ridiculous hour. "Don't you know any better than to go out without any umbrella? What's the matter with you?" Holding the door open, he urged her to come in out of the rain.

"Do you think I have any chance at all?"

He rubbed his eyes and she followed him into the one room that served as his living room, dining room, and bedroom. She shed her soaked sweater and grabbed a towel from the bathroom to dry her hair.

"You might win. Lots of people win cases for the

wrong reasons. You never know how a judge will rule. What you have going against you is that you are a single parent with very limited resources. The court really doesn't care if Brad is dead, or if you never even knew the father's name. I'm sure that Chris and Matt's lawyer will point out that the baby is illegitimate, and they'll try to use that against you. The judge will consider the unfortunate circumstances of Brad's death, but the fact remains that you are alone. You haven't been working long enough to have established a solid employment record and a steady income. Matt and Chris are settled, they both have good jobs, and they have held up their end of the bargain by providing a good home for your son. On the other hand, you are the birth mother, and in some judge's minds, many in fact, that counts for everything." He didn't tell her anything she didn't already know, and hadn't already considered.

"I'm afraid."

"You should be, I told you that today. If you lose, you lose big time, and I think that would be very hard for you to accept. Harder for you than dealing with what you have already done. Plus, as I said before, I think you've made a bad call starting this process at all."

She began to cry, long heavy sobs that told how difficult all of this had been.

"Oh Kerry, please, please try to be reasonable. You're making a terrible mistake. Just let him go and get on with it."

"Don't lecture me anymore. Stop trying to make me change my mind. I told you what I am going to do and that's it. If you're really my friend, you'll just hold me and help me through this," she sobbed, falling into his open arms.

He took her and held her to him. "I will help you through this, in any way I can, but don't expect me to change my mind."

She managed to stop crying, and tried to think only about how good it felt to be in his arms. He stroked her hair and face until her tears dried, then he lifted her face to his and caressed her as he had tried to do once before. Only this time she responded in a manner more urgent than his own. He led her over to his rumpled bed, and finally they were naked in each other's arms. Words were meaningless as they made love with a desperate intensity. When they had exhausted each other, she curled up with her back to him, and he planted a thousand tiny kisses on her shoulders. He was happy, and sated, and had never been so delighted that he didn't have an eight o'clock class that morning. Now they could sleep peacefully for a few hours in each other's arms. But the moment he closed his eyes Kerry wriggled out of his embrace and sat up in bed.

"Where are you going?" he asked sleepily.

"Work," she answered, throwing back the covers and allowing the cold air to sweep across Josh's naked body. He reached out and tried to pull her back to him, but she was too quick and all he was able to retrieve was the sheet.

"Kerry, it's early. Come back here. You know that no one shows up at the office much before ten."

"Not me," she shot back as she tried to locate her

clothes in the pile they had created by the bed. She separated her things, tossed Josh's aside, and continued her search. "I want to get in there as soon as possible. I'm in terrible trouble with Gretchen as it is, and this is certainly no time to lose my job. Imagine what my chances will be of getting the baby back if I don't even have a job."

"Kerry, you're not still thinking of going ahead with this crazy idea, are you?"

She stopped midway through pulling up her jeans, and turned to him. "Are you kidding? What kind of question is that? Of course I'm going ahead with it. What did you think was going to happen, that I would get up this morning and want to rush back down to the courthouse to retrieve my letter? To pretend that this was just a lark and that once again I've changed my mind? Not on your life. It's too important to me, and besides, I've started the process, there's no turning back now. In fact, the sooner I know the date of the hearing, the happier I'll be."

"Okay, Kerry, if that's what you want, I have to wish you luck. I hope everything goes as you planned. I'd like to see you happy, but I still can't agree with you."

"And I'm not asking you to," she said, ready to leave. Suddenly she felt very sad that he couldn't support her, because she treasured his friendship. But not enough to give up on what she knew she had to do. "All I'm asking is for you to be my friend."

"Good luck, Kerry," he said dismissively, turning his head back to his pillow instead of kissing her good-bye.

She closed the door quietly as she left, and for a moment she was torn between running back to the comfort of Josh's bed and beginning to fight the biggest battle of her life. For a moment she stood outside, her hand still on the doorknob, then she headed off into the thick fog toward her apartment.

Chapter 27

Lisbeth's reaction to her decision to stop the adoption was equally as negative as Josh's. The only difference was that instead of yelling at her, she merely shook her head sadly. Kerry had asked if they could have dinner together, and she had waited until their coffee had been served before breaking the news to her.

"Oh, dear," Lisbeth said when she finally spoke, "I do hope you know what you're doing."

"I do, Grandmother. All I really am sure of is that I can't stop thinking about him, and how much I want to be with him."

"I don't think this is going to be easy. I'm sure Chris and Matt are going to put up a fight. And that lawyer of theirs, that awful man, will surely make it very rough for you."

"I'm aware of that, and all I can do is be honest and hope that the judge will rule in my favor. I am the baby's mother," she repeated, as if it were a mantra.

The one thing Lisbeth knew for certain was that Kerry was more determined than ever. She had no choice but to support her as best she could, even though she thought her granddaughter was making a terrible mistake. "Well, I suppose if you're going to go through with this we had better find someone to represent you. Have you spoken to any attorneys?"

"No, I've decided not to. I can represent myself as well as anyone. I chose not to have anyone for the preliminary work, and I don't think I need anyone now. I know that Mike Salter can be a monster, but he would be that way regardless of whether I had my own attorney or not. I'm going to prepare for the worst, and try to be as honest and convincing as I can possibly be. After all, I am the child's mother, and the adoption is not yet finalized. I'm counting on those two facts to be enough for me to get the baby back."

"Kerry, I don't agree with any of this, I've made that very clear, but if it's what you want I will try to help you in any way I can. That's all I can do."

"And that's all I want from you. Will you testify for me at the hearing?"

Lisbeth hesitated. "I will, dear, if I am called to, but I will have to tell the truth. It's an odd situation, because I know Chris and Matt so well, but I'll do the best I can for you."

"Thank you, Grandmother. I'll let you know when I hear from the court. We should be put on the calendar as soon as the Social Services person completes her report. She's scheduled to visit me next week. After that she'll see Chris and Matt and she will file a report. That report will be crucial to the judge's decision. I'm going to try my best to convince her that my apartment is adequate for the baby. It may not be as big or as nicely furnished as theirs, but it will do just fine. I have a job, and I can afford to care for him. I just hope she sees it the same way."

"So do I, dear, so do I." Lisbeth sounded weary, and they paid the check and left.

Kerry spent the next week trying to make her apartment appear to be the perfect place to raise a child. She bought loads of stuffed animals at Macy's and decorated the living room with them. She had bears, and lions, and toy fire trucks—every toy a little boy might want—even though at six months Shelby was far too young to play with most of the things she'd bought. No matter, she thought, it would show the woman that she was already thinking ahead for the future. She put the pictures Chris had given her all over the apartment. She bought a crib and sheets and towels for him. She went to a bookstore and bought manuals on child rearing. She marked many of the pages with Post-it notes and displayed the books on the table next to her bed. She bought a case of formula and lined the cans up on the counter in the kitchen. There would be no doubt in any social worker's mind that she was ready for the baby.

•   •   •

Two days before the Social Services worker was scheduled to visit, Kerry, as had become her new habit, went to the
office early. When she arrived she was surprised to see three
men she didn't know huddled in Gretchen's office. Gretchen
never held meetings at seven-thirty in the morning. And who
were these men? she wondered.

She headed straight for her cubicle, but moments later
she heard Gretchen ushering the men out. Unable to hide
her curiosity, she went over to her boss.

"That's the earliest I've ever seen you in a meeting,"
Kerry said, finding her at the coffee machine. "What's up?"
She filled her own cup and then looked up at Gretchen. One
look at her face told her something was wrong. "Can I help?"
she asked.

"Well, Kerry, as long as you're the first one in, I might
as well begin with you. But after our conversation you must
go back to your desk, and continue to work until I tell you
otherwise. All right?"

"Yes of course, Gretchen, whatever you say," Kerry
replied, as she followed her to her office.

They both sat, and Gretchen took a long sip of coffee
before she spoke. "Kerry, the magazine has been sold. It's not
good news. We've been bought by a big publisher in New
York, and this office is being eliminated. After next week
Gardens & Homes will no longer exist in San Francisco. The
office will be closed and all work will be done back east. In a
nutshell, we're all out of jobs."

It took only a second for Kerry to understand the impact of what Gretchen was saying. Her position at *Gardens & Homes* was more than just a job to her, it was a means of getting her baby back. Without it she didn't have a chance in the world of succeeding. What judge would grant her custody of a child if she didn't even have a job? Her world suddenly closed in around her, and she felt as hopeless and frightened as she had ever been.

"I'm trying to work out some severance for all of you, but I don't know how generous they're going to be. I'm sorry, Kerry. You've been so helpful here, but I know that you'll be able to find another job. It might take some time, but you will. And of course you can count on my help. And Lisbeth will be fine too, don't worry about her. The new owners want her to continue her column."

"That's good," she managed to say. "When will the office be closing?"

"I'm going to try to keep it open until next Wednesday. At least that will give us time to pack up all the files."

"So soon."

"Yes, the new issue is almost finished, and the new people can handle whatever is left to do. Well, that's it for now. Please don't say anything to anyone yet. I want to tell each member of the staff myself."

She left Gretchen's office and immediately went downstairs to the newsstand. She bought the morning papers, returned to her desk, and began searching through the help wanted ads. The clock was ticking, and already it looked as if she was out of time.

•   •   •

When Kerry heard the doorbell and went to greet the Social Services worker, she prayed that the woman wouldn't ask her about her job. In the past two days she had responded to forty-two ads in the newspaper, had visited three temp agencies, and had registered at four employment agencies. So far no one had offered her a job, not even a temporary assignment.

The social worker, Sally Anderson, was a plainly dressed woman with a brusque manner. She refused Kerry's offer of tea or fruit juice. She removed her pad from her tote bag, and immediately began her investigation.

"Please make yourself at home," Kerry suggested.

"Don't worry, I will. Just give me a few minutes to look around here."

"If you have any questions, I'll be happy to answer them."

"Don't worry, I'm not shy."

Kerry tried to relax as the woman walked around the small apartment, opening closet doors, looking around, then making notes on her pad. Kerry would give anything to see what the woman was writing.

"Miss McKinney, do you work during the day?"

"Yes, I do." She wasn't lying. Until Wednesday she was still employed.

"What do you plan to do with the child during these hours?"

"I have arranged for someone to come in and take care of him while I am gone. He will remain in the house. No day-care."

"I see. And can you afford that on your salary?"

"I get some help from a relative. My grandmother," she added, wanting to sound as cooperative as possible.

"I see," she repeated. "Miss McKinney, do you date?"

"Date?"

"Yes, do you see men?"

"Not really, no."

"You do not have any dates? You don't go out with men?"

"Well, I have one special friend." Even though Josh wasn't talking to her she still thought that was an accurate way of referring to him.

"And does he spend the night here sometimes?"

"No. No he doesn't."

"And do you sometimes spend the night at his house, or apartment?"

"Yes, I have in the past." The woman continued writing. "But of course, once the baby comes I certainly won't be doing that."

"Of course."

Kerry felt the interview wasn't going very well, but she didn't know what to say to make it better.

"Well, I think that's all," Ms. Anderson announced, as she made her way toward the door.

"Isn't there anything else you'd like to know? I'd be

happy to tell you whatever it might be," she said. "I really want my baby back."

Ms. Anderson seemed not to hear her last comment. "No, I've seen it all, and now I'll do my report. Save your comments for the judge. You'll have plenty of time to talk at the hearing."

"Yes, I hope so. Well, good night then."

"Good night, Miss McKinney."

Kerry stood by the window and watched Miss Anderson disappear into the darkness. Her visit hadn't done much to boost Kerry's confidence. In fact, now she was more worried than ever.

"I'm sure you've read in the papers that it hasn't been a very good year for retailers," the woman said. "Usually we are able to keep some of our Christmas help, but this year we had to let everyone go right after the January sales. So I'm sorry, I really have nothing to offer you."

But she had to, Kerry insisted. This was her last chance, her last hope of getting a job before the hearing. Aware that the retail business was a disaster, she still set out determined that some store must need an attractive young woman to sell their merchandise. But store after store had told her no, not right now. Nordstrom's personnel office wouldn't even let her fill out an application, Neiman Marcus told her to call them next fall, and many of the small boutiques along the side streets around Union Square were being staffed by their owners. So she had finally ended up at Macy's, where she had camped out in the personnel office for nearly four hours, until she could catch someone's attention. She had approached a kind-looking woman and practically begged to speak with her. Now she sat in her office, hearing the same old story. There simply were no positions available.

"Kerry, you said that your magazine was sold, and that the office was closed. Have you considered going on unemployment, until you find something else? In this situation you're perfectly entitled to it."

She was trying to be helpful, but Kerry's patience was running out. She was up against a deadline, and she had to have a job. If the judge heard that she had filed for unemployment she would never get her baby back.

"I know that, Mrs. Halpern," she said. "But I really don't want to go that route. I need a real job. I'll do any kind of work—stock help, the restaurant, housekeeping—there must be something available in the housekeeping department. Please, I'll do whatever you ask."

The woman looked at her kindly, but merely shook her head. "I'm sorry, there just—"

This was Kerry's last chance; she had nothing to lose. "Mrs. Halpern, I have a baby, a little son, I have to take care of him. Please, I need a job."

Mrs. Halpern picked up a thick report from her desk, and began leafing through the pages.

Kerry held her breath.

"Well, there is one possibility," she began, "but it's not on the selling floor, and it's certainly not glamorous."

"I'll take it, it doesn't matter what it is."

"You better wait until I tell you. It's working in the beauty salon, cleaning up after the hairdressers. It's not an assistant's position, so you won't be cutting hair or shampooing anyone. It's strictly housekeeping. You'll be asked to keep many different people happy in a very busy environment. It can be hard work. The salon is closed on Mondays, so that would be your regular day off."

"I'll do it, I'm sure I can do it. When can I start?"

"Well, we need to do some paperwork, and process it through the system. How about a week from Monday?"

"Can't I start sooner than that? How about tomorrow?"

"Kerry, I can't turn the paperwork around that fast. I have to tell the salon, and they might want to meet with you. Usually they trust me on things like this, but you never know."

"I understand, but how about Thursday, then? I could be here first thing Thursday morning."

Mrs. Halpern smiled. "All right, all right, be here at nine on Thursday, and I'll take you upstairs and introduce you to the salon staff. Welcome, Kerry, I know you'll do just fine."

"I will. Thank you, Mrs. Halpern. I can't tell you how much this means to me." And for the first time in her life she hugged a perfect stranger.

She practically danced out of the building. She had a new job. And when that monster Mike Salter asked her if she was employed she could say yes, and it would be true. Sure, she would only have been at it for less than a week, but they shouldn't penalize her for that.

It was Tuesday night. The hearing was only six days away.

Chapter 28

Lisbeth and Kerry arrived at the courthouse early, and when they finally found the room where the hearing would take place, the first person they saw was Elaine. She motioned them over to where they were supposed to sit. Seeing her comforted Kerry, for Elaine had been there for her from the very beginning, never wavering in her commitment to stand by Kerry, no matter what her decision. They were already settled by the time Chris and Matt entered, accompanied, of course, by Mike Salter. They were all beautifully dressed. Chris looked especially lovely in a subdued navy suit with a big shawl draped around her shoulders. Matt wore a dark suit as well, and they looked like successful people who were able to give a child a wonderful, loving home. They glanced in Kerry's direction, but did not acknowledge her. Lisbeth waved slightly, then patted Kerry's hand in encouragement. Suddenly Kerry was sorry that she had chosen a bright red dress for the occasion. She should have worn something that looked less festive, something more serious. But it was too late now. The proceedings would begin as soon as Judge Wenner arrived.

Kerry was glad that this was only a hearing. Elaine had explained that although it was similar to a trial, it wouldn't be as formal or intimidating. Still, each side would have a chance to speak and ask questions, and then it would be up to the judge to make a ruling. It could take as little as two days, or as long as a month to reach a decision.

Kerry looked around the room for the Social Services worker, but she was nowhere in sight. The only other person there was the court reporter, who sat by her machine.

She watched as Mike Salter began to shuffle papers around, and for the second time that morning she doubted her own judgment. Maybe she should have taken Lisbeth's advice and hired an attorney of her own. Then she would have someone to turn to, someone to protect her when Mike Salter began his attack. Again, it was too late now. No, she reminded herself, she held the highest card—she was the baby's birth mother. Nothing in the world could change that.

The door opened and Judge Roslyn Wenner entered. Elaine had told her that Judge Wenner had been on the bench for nearly thirty years, and her colleagues admired and respected her. She ran a tight ship but was generally acknowledged to be a fair person. She surveyed the room in one sweeping glance and motioned for everyone to sit.

Since Kerry had initiated the proceedings, she spoke first. She rose slowly and faced the judge.

"I have put my life together since I gave birth," Kerry said in as controlled and steady a voice as she could muster. "And now I am in a position to take care of my child. I am his mother and there is no one in the world who loves him more than I do. I made a mistake, a terrible mistake, and I hope that I will not be punished for that mistake for the rest of my life."

"Thank you, Ms. McKinney. I'm sure you have some questions, Mr. Salter."

"Yes, Your Honor, I do."

Kerry took a deep breath. She knew this would be the toughest part of the hearing. Elaine had coached her—be sincere, be succinct, and whatever happens, don't let the bastard get to you.

"Ms. McKinney, I haven't seen you since you were in the hospital. How are you?" The lawyer sounded like a snake charmer, but Kerry knew better than to relax.

"Fine, thank you."

"Good. I would like to recall our last conversation. I believe you had decided not to go forward with the adoption the day after the baby was born. Is that correct?"

"Yes, it is."

"And then, I believe, the next day you changed your mind, and decided that you would, after all, sign the release papers. Is that right?"

"Yes, it is, and I did."

"Now you have decided, after nearly six months, to ask for the baby to be given back to you, is that correct?"

"Yes."

"What made you change your mind once again?"

"As I told the court in my letter and in my statement today, I have put my life in order, and now I can take care of him. Before I felt that I wasn't in a position to do that."

"I see, and what exactly has changed since then?"

"I have my own apartment, and a job."

"A job. What do you do?"

"I work for Macy's."

"In what capacity?"

"I work in the beauty salon."

"Are you a stylist in that salon?"

"No, I am a housekeeper."

"How long have you been doing this?"

"One week," she practically whispered.

"One week, I see," he said, walking around the table. Judge Wenner looked confused.

"So, since you have been employed for a week you feel you are ready to care for your baby. Is that correct?"

"No, it's not. I mean, it is correct that I can take care of my child, but not because I have had a job for one week. I had another job before that, a good one, at a magazine, but I was let go." Immediately she regretted having used those words.

"Let go, you mean you were fired?"

"No, the company was sold. They let everyone go."

"And that job, how long did you have it?"

"Five months." She lowered her head; he was beginning to get to her.

"Let's move on and talk about who's going to take care of your child while you are at the hair salon. What are your plans?"

"I will hire someone to come to the house while I am at work. Just like Chris and Matt do now."

"I am not concerned right now with the Brookses and what they do, Ms. McKinney. I am only interested in you. But since you mentioned it, I would like to point out to the court that Mrs. Brooks has reduced her work schedule so that she is able to spend more time at home with Shelby. She now works at home at least two or three days each week."

Once again Kerry could have kicked herself—if she hadn't brought it up, Mike Salter would never have been able to say that. It was shocking news to Kerry, and only hurt her case even more.

"Ms. McKinney, I would like to ask you a few questions about your past, and about the baby's father, Brad Evans. How long did you know the father?"

She had to think for a moment. "We grew up together. So for all my life."

"I see, and I understand that you were planning to marry him."

"Yes, I was, but he was killed."

"Yes, I understand that. But the question was, were you planning to marry him?"

"Yes."

"And were you officially engaged to be married?"

"Yes."

"When did that happen?"

"At Christmas year before last."

"And when did you discover that you were pregnant?"

"The following March."

"What did Brad say about the fact that you were pregnant?"

"I never told him. I never had a chance."

"Are you saying that Brad never knew he was going to be a father?"

"That's right."

"Brad was killed in a car accident, is that correct?"

"Yes, it is."

"And when did that tragedy occur?"

"In April, he died on April seventh."

"Let me see if I understand it correctly. You found out that you were pregnant in March, and yet when he died on April seventh, a month later, you still hadn't had a chance to tell him?"

"No, he was away."

"He was away? Where was he? Out of the country, unreachable?"

"No, he was in Los Angeles."

"And you were in Carson City, Nevada. I see, thank you very much, Ms. McKinney."

He turned back toward his seat, and Kerry thought the worst was over. But just as he reached Chris and Matt, he turned back and faced her again.

"Oh, please, just one more thing, Ms. McKinney. How

often did you visit your son after he went home with the Brookses?"

"I went just before Christmas. I took him some toys."

"At Christmas, all right. And were there other visits?"

"No."

"So between September and December you only visited your son once. Was that because you felt you were not welcome at Chris and Matt's?"

"No, it wasn't that at all. Chris said I could come any time I wanted."

"Thank you, Ms. McKinney. That's it for now."

Kerry wanted to say more, she wanted to explain why she had waited to tell Brad in person, and how it was too painful to visit the baby knowing that she would have to leave him, but the judge suggested they take a break. Kerry was crushed. Mike Salter had led her down a path, and she had followed him like an animal to slaughter.

The rest of the morning passed in a haze as Matt and Chris presented their side of the story. Yes, they loved baby Shelby as if he had been born to them. Yes, the two of them spent every possible moment with him, he was the joy of their luxurious, well-ordered lives, and they would be devastated if he was ever taken from them. Why, they had already begun his college fund, Chris said, wiping a tear from her eye.

The judge listened intently but impassively, and at the end of the session she asked Kerry if she wanted to make a closing statement. Kerry rose again and repeated what she had said earlier, but she was drained from the questioning, and her voice wasn't nearly as strong as it had been earlier. Mike Salter declined the judge's invitation, saying that he had nothing to add to Chris's and Matt's heartfelt declarations. Judge Wenner thanked them all and told them that she would begin considering their case and when she had ruled they would be notified of her decision by mail.

Kerry, Lisbeth, and Elaine waited until everyone had left the room before gathering up their things.

"I think they're probably gone by now, dear," Lisbeth said, guiding Kerry out into the hallway. She knew that if Kerry saw Mike Salter she wouldn't be able to control herself, and she could hardly blame her.

But they hadn't waited quite long enough. Mike and Matt were standing on the steps of the courthouse apparently waiting for Chris.

Kerry heard Mike say, "Well, I think we did it. Trust me, you won't have any regrets fighting this, and if we have to, we can always appeal."

"The only regret I have is the day I met that girl," she heard Matt reply.

Kerry declined Elaine's invitation for an early lunch, preferring to walk from the courthouse to Macy's. She was due at one, and then faced a long day of sweeping hair and cleaning out sinks. She needed some fresh air and some time to think. She kissed Lisbeth on the cheek.

"Thank you for coming, Grandmother. It really helped, having you there."

"I'll always be there for you, no matter what," she said,

convinced that it had gone badly for Kerry. Very badly indeed. Mike Salter had begun to deliver on his promise. "Now all we can do is wait, dear," she added, not wanting to encourage any false hopes Kerry might still have.

"It seems endless already," Kerry agreed. "We can only hope that motherhood will win out." She smiled and started off toward Union Square.

"You sure walk fast," he said, when he finally caught up with her.

Kerry was lost in her thoughts, replaying in her mind what had happened that morning. Josh's voice startled her. "Oh, hi, where did you come from?"

"I've been trying to catch up with you since you left Lisbeth at the courthouse," he explained, "but you've been moving at such a fast clip I practically had to run to catch up. Didn't you hear me calling your name?"

"No, of course not or I would have stopped. I'm walking so fast because I don't want to be late. I have to be at the store by one. And I was just thinking about the hearing."

"Well, how did it go?" he asked.

She wanted to ask him what difference it made to him, since he didn't support her anyway, but the look on his face said that he was truly concerned about her.

"Oh, I think very badly for me. It was exactly as you said it would be. Mike Salter was prepared to bury me, and I think he probably succeeded. He asked me questions about

Brad that made it sound as if I was hiding the pregnancy from him. I didn't have a chance to explain that I wanted to tell him in person. But that wasn't the worst. He brought up the fact that I've only been to visit Shelby once, and I think the judge wondered why, if I was so interested in getting him back, I didn't go more often. It's a good question, and it's difficult to explain how I felt about going there. And then of course he asked all about my job, and that was the part that sounded the worst. It just didn't make me sound very stable."

"I know, I'm really sorry about the magazine. After I heard, I called you to tell you how terrible I felt, and to see if there was anything I could do to help you. In fact, I called you several times. You must have been too busy looking for a new job to call me back."

It was true, she hadn't returned his calls, and now she felt guilty. "You're right and I owe you an apology. I only had a week to find a new job, and it isn't such a great time to be looking. I practically had to beg for the one I finally got. And it's barely going to pay the rent. But thanks for thinking of me."

They continued walking toward downtown, and once the store was in sight, Kerry began to relax a bit. Suddenly it occurred to her that it wasn't just a coincidence that Josh had been waiting outside the courtroom. "By the way, how did you know the hearing was this morning?"

"My mom told me."

"Gretchen told you?" she repeated, shocked to hear that his mother knew what she had avoided telling her for so many months. "How did she know?"

"One guess, Kerry. Lisbeth told her. I'm sorry if you think your grandmother revealed a deep, dark secret, but Gretchen is her best friend. They've both been through a lot together, with Charles and all, and now with you. I really don't think you realize how hard this has been on Lisbeth. She tried so hard to help you, to get you through this tough time, and I think this court hearing was really bothering her. She's in a very difficult position, especially being friends with Chris and Matt, and having them right upstairs. Charles has also been having problems again. She wanted everything to work out, and now it's all blown up again. I guess she just needed someone to talk to. So when I asked Mom about you she said the hearing was scheduled for nine this morning. And I wanted to be there for you, even though you've been ignoring me. So here I am."

She was happy that he had come. It was the sign of a true friend to be supportive even though he disagreed with what you were doing. She leaned over and kissed him. He took her in his arms and hugged her.

"I miss you," he said. "And I hope the judge rules in your favor, if that's what you really want."

"Thank you, I appreciate that. Now I had better run or risk losing this menial job I talked my way into."

"Dinner tonight?"

She hesitated, but only for a moment. "Yes . . . yes, that would be very nice." They kissed again and then she walked through the side entrance, feeling much better than she had all morning.

Chapter 29

During the next two weeks, Kerry and Josh spent almost every evening together. He would drive down to the store to pick her up after work, and she would emerge looking pale and exhausted.

"You can't believe how much hair there is in the world. And most of it is on me," she laughed, brushing off her shirt and sweater. He was proud of her for keeping her spirits so high while working such an awful job.

Kerry now insisted on stopping by her apartment before they went out. Blocks before they arrived, she would have her mailbox key in her hand. She would jump out of the car even before Josh had had a chance to put it in park, and then run frantically toward the front door and her mailbox. He would remain in the car, watching her sort through junk mail and bills, looking for an envelope with a state seal.

At the end of the second week, which had been an agony for her, he saw that the news had arrived. She rushed back to the car, waving it wildly.

She ripped open the envelope and read in silence. He waited, no longer even certain what he hoped for her. If she won the case, she would be euphoric, but she would also be facing a difficult future, the constant struggle of a life as a single parent. If she lost, she would be heartbroken, and he wasn't certain that his love for her, as powerful as it was, would be enough to help her overcome the loss she would feel. He held his breath, but when he heard her scream in delight, he knew that in the judge's mind biological motherhood triumphed.

"I won," she cried through her tears. "I won. I can pick the baby up on Saturday. And it says in the letter that Matt and Chris will not appeal the decision. I have to call and arrange the time with Chris, but he's going to be coming home. Oh, I can't believe it."

One look at Josh's expression told her that, as much as he loved her, he couldn't share her happiness. "Josh, please try to be happy for me. Please, he's my son."

"I told you that I didn't agree with you, but because it is what you wanted so much, I am glad the judge ruled for you. Now I only hope—"

"I know what you're going to say. You only hope I can handle it. I will, I know I can. Now don't ruin it for me. Let's go out and celebrate."

He took her to her favorite restaurant, and they sat at the table she liked best. As hard as he tried, Josh could not force himself into a celebratory mood. He couldn't help thinking about the changes that inevitably would occur in their relationship, and how Kerry would now be devoting all her energy to her son. He felt selfish thinking these things, but during the past two weeks he had allowed himself to dream about a future in which he and Kerry had children of their own.

"Kerry, I'm going to go home tonight, I'm really tired," he said, kissing her good night at the door of her apartment instead of going in and spending the night with her as he had done so often lately.

"Just one more thing. I still haven't changed my mind about this, and I want you to know that I'm not certain if our relationship can go on the way it has been. That will make me very sad, because I love you and want to be with you. But you're doing something I think is terribly wrong. I think you should consider once more what this will do to Matt and Chris. The pain they are experiencing now is certainly just as powerful as your happiness."

She stood in the doorway and shook her head, but he wasn't really certain if she'd even heard him, let alone understood him. She was still too overcome with joy for what he had said to matter.

Saturday was still two days away, and Kerry was convinced that she was going to feel every minute tick by until she was expected at the Brookses. She had one very brief, terse conversation with Chris, in which they had agreed that Shelby would be ready to be picked up at ten o'clock in the morning.

She was up at six on Saturday. Now all she had to do was wait a few hours. For the first time she considered what Chris and Matt must be going through. One thing Chris said was that the only reason they weren't appealing the decision was that they thought it would be harmful for the baby to remain with them for months, maybe even as long as a year, and then possibly be taken away. She wanted Kerry to know that no matter how painful this had been, her foremost concern was, and had always been, for the baby. Kerry couldn't help but think of what Josh had said. He was right, she had broken up a family, and she had caused a great deal of pain for the one person who had helped her so much. Lisbeth had sounded so weary and sad when she'd called her with the news. Well, she couldn't dwell on that now. It was time to bring Shelby home.

It was raining hard by the time she reached the Brookses, so she told the taxi driver to wait. "I'll only be a minute, so please don't leave," she said, as she got out of the cab. When she got to the front door she hesitated before knocking. Suddenly she remembered the last time she had been here, carrying presents for the little boy. She recalled the look of pure bliss on Chris's face, as they leaned over the crib and admired the sleeping newborn.

"Go ahead, pick him up," she'd said. "I'll be standing by with a bottle."

Kerry had heard such love in her voice, such devotion and caring. At the hearing Chris had said that she always thought of him as her son, and as the best gift she had ever been given in her life.

Kerry knocked lightly, and as she heard footsteps approach, she felt her resolve fading.

Chris opened the door and the vision that Kerry had of

her, of a beautiful, honest woman who had loved her baby as if it had been born to her, vanished. Chris's hair, rather than being loose and framing her face, was tied back in a ponytail. She wore no makeup and her eyes were red and swollen. She had an old sweatsuit on that should have been discarded ages ago. Kerry had never seen her in anything so ratty.

She ran her hands back through her hair, and nervously tightened the band, which held her ponytail. "I'm sorry, please forgive how I look. It's just that since we heard the decision I haven't really left the house. I wanted to spend as much time . . ." She started to cry and she reached into her pocket for a tissue. "I'm sorry," she said, motioning Kerry into the hallway. "I promised myself that I wouldn't do this."

Behind her, in a car carrier on the floor, was baby Shelby. He was wrapped in a blanket with lions on it, and he wore a tiny baseball cap to protect him from the rain. A bag of diapers and more toys was by the side of the carrier. Chris had thought of everything, and she had done it with love and concern. She wanted the baby to get to his new home with the least disturbance possible.

Kerry stared at the beautiful infant. Her heart was in her throat, but she knew now what she had to do. For a moment she couldn't take her eyes off him. He was so much bigger than she remembered.

"Chris, I'm not taking the baby. He's yours. He's been yours from the day you brought him home. I made a promise to you, and it's taken me until this moment to be able to keep it. I can't take him from you. I know now that it's not the right thing to do."

Chris stared at her in amazement. She was torn between hugging her and striking her. They had been through so much she didn't know if she could trust her at all.

"Kerry, you don't mean it. You said that the last time, and then you changed your mind and put us through such hell—you can't imagine what it's been like. So now you've won your fight, and he's yours. Please take him."

Kerry began to cry. "I can't, Chris. It's the wrong thing to do. I can see that now. He's yours, and you've given him so much. No, I'm not going to take him, and I promise you I will never change my mind again. Not for the rest of my life. I'm sorry for all the pain I've caused you, and I hope someday you will be able to forgive me. I will want to see him sometime, and I'll always want to hear how he is doing, but I will never fight you again for him. Just promise me that you will keep loving him as you do now."

Chris was no longer in doubt. Kerry had not come to take the baby. She hugged her tightly and through her tears she thanked her for deciding to let him stay.

Once her tears had subsided, Kerry bent down and gently stroked the baby's cheek, and then she left. On her way down she stopped off at Lisbeth's to tell her what she had done, and to cry a few more tears for the baby who would not be going home with her.

Epilogue

The memorial service for Brad was scheduled for late March. Coach was responsible for planning the event. During the ceremony they would retire his old number and at the same time announce the winner of the scholarship fund, which had been set up in his memory. It would be given to a student who excelled both academically as well as in the sport of his choice.

"You must come," Nancy had said. "You've been away far too long, and it's very important that you be here. Everyone has been asking about you."

"I wouldn't miss it for anything," she had agreed. "But I want Josh to come with me. Then he can meet everyone and see where I went to school. I can give him the deluxe ten-minute tour around Carson City, and take him for a steak at Cutler's."

"He will be more than welcome. And try to drag Lisbeth along if you can."

Lisbeth had declined, so just the two of them set off in Josh's car. Kerry hadn't been home in nearly a year. She looked wistfully out the window when they passed through Tahoe as they headed toward the Nevada border.

"You okay?" Josh asked, reaching over and taking her hand.

"Yes, I'm doing just fine," she said, meaning it, but knowing how much more difficult this would be without him. Every day, she was thankful for his presence in her life. He had taught her many things, but most of all he had made her believe in herself and in her future. And in their future together. From the day she had decided to leave the baby with Chris and Matt he had been more attentive and loving than ever. He was patient with her, and didn't push her to make any commitments to him. More than anything he wanted to be sure she was ready, and he was willing to wait until she was able to take the next step.

The service was short but very moving. The auditorium was packed, and as they raised Brad's old jersey up to join those of the school's other heroes, everyone cheered wildly. Then Coach spoke, remembering Brad as a second son, and one hell of a football player. Then the principal announced the recipient of the first Bradly Eric Evans Memorial Scholarship Fund. Kerry winced when she heard his name: he had hated to be called Bradley, hated it with a passion, and she used to be able to get him to do almost anything if she promised not to utter his given name.

To thunderous applause, the deserving student came forward to receive his award, and on that positive note the ceremony ended. But before he left the hall, the principal offered the group a closing thought. "As we turn toward the future, let us not ever forget our past, but learn what we can from it. We must not let the memories be a burden to us, just a joyous reminder for our past blessings."

Kerry squeezed Josh's hand and looked over at him. "I'll buy that," she said.